Room Swept Home

Also by Remica Bingham-Risher

Wesleyan Poetry

Remica Bingham-Risher

ROOM

SWEPT

HOME

Wesleyan University Press / Middletown, Connecticut

Wesleyan University Press
Middletown CT 06459
www.wesleyan.edu/wespress

Manufactured in the United States of America
Designed and composed in Garamond Premier Pro by Mindy Basinger Hill

Library of Congress Cataloging-in-Publication Data

Names: Bingham-Risher, Remica, author.
Title: Room swept home / Remica Bingham-Risher.
Other titles: Room swept home (Compilation)
Description: Middletown, Connecticut : Wesleyan University Press, 2024. |
    Series: Wesleyan poetry | Includes bibliographical references. | Summary:
    "Poetry exploring the impacts of family bonds through enslavement and
    institutionalization in the stories of three generations of women, examining
    race and lineage, and asking: What do we inherit at the core of our fractured
    living?" — Provided by publisher.
Identifiers: LCCN 2023036720 (print) | LCCN 2023036721 (ebook) |
    ISBN 9780819500984 (hardcover) | ISBN 9780819500991 (ebook)
Subjects: BISAC: POETRY / American / African American & Black |
    FICTION / African American & Black / Women | LCGFT: Poetry.
Classification: LCC PS3602.I544 R66 2024 (print) | LCC PS3602.I544 (ebook) |
    DDC 811/.6—dc23/eng/20230822
LC record available at https://lccn.loc.gov/2023036720
LC ebook record available at https://lccn.loc.gov/2023036721

5   4   3   2   1

For my Nana, Shirley Bingham,
who shared her memories of Minnie with me
and loves hard enough to make us believe
grandmothers are our best thing.

and

For Aunt Mary (Evelyn) Brown,
Mary's oldest child, who made it here
unscathed, who shares her own stories
and encourages me always.

I just know I could if I knowed how to write, and had a little learning
I could put off a book on this here situation.

MINNIE LEE FOWLKES, 1937

Contents

WHAT SURVIVED

Lost Friends.

NOTE. – We receive many letters asking about lost friends. All such letters will be published in this column from the end of the Civil War until those in need stop looking and, if this isn't the case, in perpetuity. We make no charge for publishing these letters from subscribers to the *Southeastern Herald*. All others enclose fifty cents to pay for publishing. Pastors will please read the requests published below from their pulpits, and report any case where friends are brought together by means of letters.

Dear Editor: I wish to inquire for the women in me, in the interest of my mother, father, aunts, uncles and a great many cousins.—I want to find my people. They were carried from us when I was less than thought of. In their dreams, they called me Seborn or Glory but now I am called Still Becoming. My parents' names are Here, Holding. Uncles names are Sprightly, Long Gone, Whisper and Roadbed; Aunts Hunger, Childfree, Childmany, Want and Wanting. My cousins are like blades of grass or kudzu and can barely be chased or named. Some were here, some are dead. Before the war, these women were held by Masters most of us have swallowed but each eve return as odd growths under our skin. Mother's mother and father's grandmother's grandmother were barely living in Petersburg, Va. They were within miles of each other and did not know blood was nearby. We heard tell before then one was bought by a family named Gee or Blackburn, the other by some called Hyman or Knight; they died and we fell to others. I was born and have not heard from them since. Friends, if you have footing on their whereabouts, please Address me at Stillwater, Va., with letters, keepsakes, any knowledge of what's come of us.

Room Swept Home

Robert Lee Bingham 1959

Shirley E. Bingham 1938

Julious C. Bingham 1934

James Bright 1912

John Bingham 1904

Rebecca Blackburn 1917

Viola R. Bingham 1908

Eddie Gee 1880

Susie Gee 1894

Minnie Lee Fowlkes 1859

Thomas Fowlkes 1869

Chloe Ann Lee 1835

Albert Lee 1830

Jesse

Caroline 1813

In the Corridor

In July 2017, my husband and I take our children to the new National Museum of African American History and Culture (NMAAHC) in Washington, DC. It has taken six months to get tickets, and the lines outside and in are still wrapped around the structure, the makeshift ropes, the Slavery and Freedom 1400–1877 exhibits. *What is left to say about slavery?* a woman asks loudly, her irritation palpable, as we make our way in. Before the trip, I've begun working on a project about my grandmothers that's been swirling in my head for years. In a strange twist of kismet, my ancestors intersect in Petersburg, Virginia, forty years before I am born. My paternal great-great-great-grandmother, Minnie Lee Fowlkes (also spelled Fulkes), lives in Petersburg and is interviewed for the Works Progress Administration (WPA) Federal Writers' Project ex-slave narratives in 1937. My maternal grandmother, Mary Etta Knight, after birthing her first child, is given a diagnosis of 'water on the brain' (postpartum was an ongoing mystery) and sent to the Central Lunatic Asylum for the Colored Insane (renamed Central State Hospital) in 1941, a stone's throw from where Minnie resides. I find this connection fascinating—two disparate women of my history, at opposite ends of their lives, converging upon the same space and time, ushering in the stretchstrain of folks who will usher in me. I know their living commences long before this confluence and am determined to search for their beginnings.

I am a poet, so I must call on history's gatekeepers (librarians and elders) to help me. They send me archives and databases, death and birth certificates, books and burial records. My inquest becomes part ethnographic, part family lore. It is difficult for most Black Americans to trace ancestors before 1865, as it is for me, so I begin looking for cultural and regional history to fill in the minutia of the times. I have traced invented psychoses, living quarters, grooming and hair rituals, faith practices, and maroons before my family and I arrive on the museum's bottom floor. I pride myself on being staunch, matter-of-fact, clear, and considered when teaching my children about even the ugliness of history. I am only teacher-mother-knower explaining artifacts from a slave ship. Teacher-mother-knower near Jefferson's ancestors, stacked as a pile of engraved bricks called the Paradox of Liberty. I turn a corner when a reconstructed slave cabin stands in front of us. I have been reading John Hope Franklin's book *Runaway Slaves: Rebels on the Plantation* and recognize the cabin's slatted wood, dark entry, and dirt floor. I am mother-daughter-brokenbird, and cry in the museum's corridor.

In early America, I am searching for what my ancestors may have seen and known. I have no illusions about finding things they might have loved because what was to love about being Black in America other than being alive? I am looking for their daily things, their living, evidence that they marked this land, were more than marked by it. I am trying to picture the physical space, so begin researching antebellum Virginia landscapes and battlefields leveled by hard-fought progress. What was bound in the trees then?

Just past the cabin at the museum, I photograph objects from a Spirit Bundle, a collection of amulets that mirrors West African traditions meant to protect passageways between physical and spiritual worlds. Because there are so many people and so little time, we have to move quickly; Reconstruction is a blur and soon we are three floors up in the modern-day galleries. I am arrested by a large visual artwork, a crown of sorts made of tools used to sculpt Black hair about which the artist, Kenya Robinson, says: "For complex reasons of race, class, gender . . . I will probably have a hair conversation with other black women for all of my days, like some kind of not-so-secret handshake of experience and history." I begin writing the poem "Commemorative Headdress For Her Journey Beyond Heaven" with all of these seemingly disparate encounters swirling in my mind. I imagine a woman who is having the route she must travel to escape the plantation braided into her hair. (I haven't found evidence of this tactic being used in the U.S.; this is just hope and imagining—though I am fascinated by the legacy of Colombia's Benkos Biho, as braiding maps into the hair of women has been reported as a tactic used to help others escape.) The poem's speaker is looking for a pathway into another world, here the swampland that will put her and her sistren out of reach, sight and mind. Writing the poem I think again about what the enslaved loved, the bundle and amulets. Of course they loved even the *thought* of freedom, the hope and wonder of it, of being together in it, a Black kind of heaven. Hence, the title of the poem is the same as that of the visual work by Robinson, with the exception of one article (*from* changed to *for*), as the poem is meant to convey the beginning of a journey, not an ending.

When we leave the museum, I look for things I've missed. Weeks later, I find a picture on my phone of thousands of well-dressed Black folk lining the streets of an unknown city with the caption "Emancipation Day Parade, 1905" and can't remember when I took it or what was nearby, so I scour historical newspapers like the *National Anti-Slavery Standard* and the *Norfolk Journal and Guide*. What I find is a great many people searching—for good omens, legal victories, justice, faith, children, joy. The *Lost Friends* column, published as early as 1866, filled full pages of each standard. Freed men and women placed the advertisements to search for others lost before or during the war. In her book *Help Me to Find My People: The African American Search for Family Lost in Slavery*, Heather Andrea Williams does the seemingly impossible work of following the trail of these ads, their impetus and a few outcomes. *The Historic New Orleans Collection*, much like *The Geography of Slavery in Virginia* (a repository of runaway slave advertisements and other documents from 1736– 1803), has digitized thousands of the columns. After reading fifty or so, I came across one by Maria Ross of Yazoo City, Mississippi, published in the *Southwestern Christian Advocate*, which began, "Dear Editor:—I want to find my people." And it breaks me open inside. It is so plain: *please help me find my people*. It cuts me to the core remembering that all folks wanted was to be together, to have someone to love and find anyone who knew to love them. The weight of my grandmothers—with all their fullness and distance—wearies and worries me. I write the poem "Lost Friends." as an imitation of the column. There is pleading, because I am desperately searching; there is birthing and blood and loss; there are figurative names that tell our stories juxtaposed against family monikers that most likely belonged to the slaveholders we are ever trying to unshackle. Something about sifting through pieces of the once-living lends itself, in my brain, to various types of abstraction. I know no matter how many details I uncover, there is still a breathing wanting left out of all I'll find. The poet's job (i.e., the poet as historian, as opposed to other undertakings such as poet as soothsayer, poet as family arbiter, poet as line dancer and the like) is to make the dead become the living. I hope this will eventually become a body of work in the voices of those journeywomen and illumine the times they endured. Perhaps, for someone in the distance, the poems will blossom and be: a Spirit Bundle, a trove or pathway, what there is left to say, an alternate kind of history.

Minnie Lee Fowlkes

(1859–1945)

Birth Story

I wasn't born on Christmas, though this is what some folks will tell you

some folks say every one born slave was born on Christmas or New Year's Day

some folks always lying, some pretend we don't know how we got here or when

but I am made of memory and the impossible long hour, I cherish every part that was mine

or my mother's, and she'd tell you too I came in the world with the sun bearing

its full heat, the day as steady as the pain—she sweat through the pallet of hay

on the floor, the dirt and rocks felt like coals underneath her—a friend there, rooted, a woman

I'd call aunt for years, gray-headed and firm, had a guiding hand the children knew

to follow, pressed on the belly, held mother's hips in place, helped her stand

when laying down wouldn't move me, found grease to ease me out with the water

and blood, and I remember what my mother said the woman told her, told me

God brought you here, God made you free   Jesus was born outdoors on a night

when the shepherds slept in the field free from frost, no snow, Christmas wasn't

his day either, but someone somewhere saw fit to give him what they thought he deserved,

what suited them, saved the truth for later

What began as an annual registration of births and deaths became the *Virginia Slave Births Index*, compiled by the Works Progress Administration (WPA). Each entry includes a child's name, birth date, mother's name, slave owner, and place of birth.

On the plantation or, as some say, *down home*

I.

We belonged to all the families.
We the blood and straw, the leaves and iron.

Children were everywhere.

Everywhere, women governed more, but men
were handed the shackle key, the collar.
Men died, we went to their women.

Daughters, widows, women held the lash.
They bartered and owed with us;
we changed hands and held.

Knee-high and wary, children carried
water to the fields,
up and down factory rows.

Little feet ran from the house
just past the trees to family land
with folded papers filled with what we didn't know.

Little eyes watched the babies
who couldn't walk the tobacco hall.

Grandmother, mother, all the same.
Mother had fifteen, and all of us sold
along with her, then some sold
from under her skirt.

Children given: one dress or cotton shirt,
no shoes, no chair or bench, just a dirt-bottom floor in the middle house,
where we wore the face we wanted,
cloistered there, mass and parcel, from day dark to night.

Pot liquor for meals on one corn cake,
    dried slab bacon on rare occasion.

A little shine on the skin, and dreaming, dreaming,
    hard fitful sleep until sun came again.

II.

Big iron pot at the meeting door
so no one would hear us holler and sing,

that's how we called unto heaven—shouting.
Some words barely words, just sound enduring.

No sound dies, just remakes itself,
willing a body, praying release from this awful thing.

Sometimes the paddy rollers—
eyes like sickly moon, cave-mouthed—

caught wind of us but vines we tied to the base of trees
would tangle up horses, fumble men.

Other times they'd enter, beat folks senseless, say
You don't have time to serve God. We brought you here

to serve us. We watched for the devil, knowing
wrath and rod would come for the wicked.

If not them, then for their children.

III.

Little pleasure in the body::

    sometimes at night she'd twirl us

or sing a song unknown   but I wasn't near grown

    when she warned me—

Blood ran

down to her ankles

the leather opened

skin of her back

an overseer   who she'd refused   tied

mother up in the barn

a block beneath her feet

an almost hanging

used a whip

like they used on horses

bathed her

in salt and water brine—

Body twisted like a doll   she knew

    pleasure must be saved

like a secret   hidden and pressed into dark::

                                          That place was full

                                              of suffering

                                          Lord, Lord—

Every part precious

    she taught me   to oil my hair   my knees::

hold on to your self   you can make your way

    through anything, you hear

anything come   it go through me

IV.

Those with visions

    (what young folks call dreams)

        knew the Bible, preached it different

said, not what white folks repeated

    Slaves, be obedient to your human masters

        with fear and trembling, in sincerity of heart,

but assured us, *You were called for freedom.*

    God spoke to some in the night

        and they told us hope would follow.

In those back days, child,

    we were never sure what the Book said.

        Couldn't read it, just trusted

in dreams until we were able with God's help

    to pull ourselves together, never lost sight

        of each other,

looked for chosen or blood kin, a path to a great big city

    with no dividing line, dreamed everyone reborn,

        running perfectly wild.

V.

I didn't know cotton
when Master Graves sold
my brother and sister
away from my mother, my grandmother,
part of them, part of us, sent down deep south

mama told me they'd have to work
in cotton country, merciless fields,
boiling sun, from first light
to when they couldn't see
their hands at night

we only knew bright leaf and Virginia,
last bit of south, tobacco in the fields,
the curing barns, the factories, the smell of it
always under our nails, in our hair

but this was better than the acres
of cotton, the backbreaking work
most powerful in myth

we never saw them again,
mother's other children,
but she worried for them,
held fast to me

Battle of the Crater

July 30, 1864

I hear a noise like wild thunder
while we are sleeping
the ground moving
near the long road maybe coming
from the trees then screaming
screaming men sounding
like a marauder band
or whatever they say on Sunday
chasing Elisha or coming after
and by the time we reach
the curing barn Mama tells me to *shush shush*
but I know what the forest sounds like
breaking I've been through a storm
and later I hear people talking
about the hole swallowing all the soldiers up
colored mostly crying
even the boy who runs
back to Miss Godsey place our place
right where we are asking for water
and it is a wide pit he says
something took the earth
and moved it and Mama says *shush*
shush when I go to ask him how
he made it here and if freedom
coming too and the boy don't
sleep that day he run before the sun
away from the fighting
and I tell Mama he left too soon
might be all those men down in the pit
touched the right bones and
looking for their friends like Elisha
after they stood up again

April when de war surrendered

But we didn't know til May cause Miss Godsey ain't said a word
    but after
we stomped and cried and made freedom songs

    Joy in the hands, joy in the feet,
even the quiet a jubilee

    Freedom sweeter than what any man say
we danced, made drums from tin and carried on
    til Sunday, til someone asked where we was heading

A whole lot of folks took off for nowhere
    other folks went looking for children
some, like me, were children but had nothing, no one
    Mama and I stayed on

Mama ain't like missus but where would we go
    that lady cried something awful,
said she'd clothe us, give us cornmeal and lard

    I worked her land and cooked, learned
to tend the garden
    and count what little was ours

Wanderlust

Where you headed?

Maybe North

Where you been?

Yonder, hard times, a street none name

Where you sleep?

In the woods, with others

Where's your kin?

Daddy left with the union, most of us scattered: everywhere

Where this road lead?

A free town

Who all over there?

Right many

Will you walk til night?

Long as I can

What you trying to find?

A mountain like a bridge

Who told you of it?

My love, in the dark

Does the road whisper now?

Whispers and sings

Are many children on it?

Some so small, they might not remember

Can we pray on that?

That and a safe journey

God come by here?

Could be a stranger, could be you Him

Strip Tobacco Like Greens

ain't much difference
    soak them in water
        to ease the leaves

then pull the largest ones
    to wrap the bundle
        these called *the hands*.

We the stemmers,
    all women on the line,
        rows filled

with traveling songs.
    I sang as a child
        at the feet of my mother,

she bound the leaves, packed
    in hogsheads.
        Some found bodies

in the large drums, put there
    for punishment, or fun.
        During the war, the factory was

a hospital, all the wounded
    gathered like cutlery,
        for a time, cared for, shined.

Work moved outdoors, never stopped.
    In the years after, we get nary
        a dollar a day, pennies

enough for those notes
    thrown wild into the field,
        low and worn

the singing from children's
　　　dancing mouths,
　　　　　those hands, like ours,

vein-heavy, softened, worked over,
　　　sweet aroma unto heaven, little more
　　　　　than ash and plenty to men.

Our mothers: upended,
　　　invented, inventors;
　　　　　our fathers: a secret,

or kept under the tally,
　　　thread woven through
　　　　　throat, groin, and spine.

Bitter stem, bitter greens,
　　　yellow leaves. Little soothes
　　　　　the busy hand, the flying mind.

Tobacco, not cotton, was king in much of Virginia. Slaves produced the majority of tobacco exported before the Civil War, and many worked with the crop well into the twentieth century. Here, mostly women sort tobacco at T. C. Williams & Co. in 1899.

Work Song

Every day the work is long   but day end gone come   we gone rise

     everything we built   everything we watered   pretty, pretty in its own time

The womb is a garden   the seeds are the body

     my hands in the land   my hands in the sea

Flood water come   leave God's children

     hand over fist   making their own wings

Every hand you see is turning   every head a heavy weight

     itching and a burning   steady growing its own face

The palm is burning   an itch means luck   pinch a nickel

     save a dollar   if it's growing   lightning struck

Sometimes up, sometimes down   sometimes level with the ground

     but journey-people   always own the wind   run with the moon   ride the clouds

What can I grow   I grow what I can   gone rest my body soon

     gone steal some sun   gone see my baby   give sugar in a silver spoon

Questions That Still Need Answering

from Questionnaire for Ex-slaves, WPA

2. Age? — (How does he know his age?)

8. Teeth?

9. Voice?

10. Eyes?

20. Master and mistress—names, number children, their names and ages?

28. Who administered punishment?

29. Manumission?

49. To whom were slaves directly responsible?

60. What was the easiest and hardest work for slaves?

74. What did slaves do when it rained?

78. How did slaves get to be house servants?

79. Where did house servants sleep?

84. Beds?

85. Beds for children?

86. Pictures?

87. Curtains?

88. Windows?

94. Was it pretty?

99. Who cooked in the quarters?

115. Who names slave babies?

123. Did they have a ring or broomstick marriage?

129. Were slaves ever divorced?

130. Describe a slave funeral?

134. Casket or coffin?

153. Did slaves ever sit down in the presence of whites?

166. Were paterollers slave owners or poor whites?

168. Was the slave code ever read to slaves?

174. Did poor whites ever beg from slaves?

175. Did free Negroes ever beg from slaves?

181. How did Negroes get free?

184. Did slaves ever get the "catching sickness"?

185. Was there ever any "bad disease" in the quarters?

186. Did doctors of midwives ever "take" slave babies?

189. Did slaves ever practice contraception?

191. Were new-born slave babies good-looking?

192. Were new-born white babies good-looking?

208. Were slaves allowed to have pencils?

215. Where did slaves sit in church?

220. What were the regular slave vacations?

224. Describe the way slaves danced?

228. What were the names of slave dances?

236. Did slaves assemble at times just to sing?

242. Did you see the stars fall?

258. Did slaves ever own watches, rings, false teeth?

278. Have you a picture of your father, mother, yourself?

281. Did you ever hear of Nat Turner? Gabriel Vesey? [*Writer seems to have confused Gabriel Prosser and Denmark Vesey.*]

283. Where were you when the war came?

310. Was the Ku [Klux] Klan in your neighborhood?

311. Was your former master in the Klan?

322. Did you or your people build a home after freedom?

Putting Mother in the Ground

December 28, 1874

Children give, children take.
I hold the baby, loud and wailing
who's just slipped out of mama,
who ferries her into the afterlife.
Daddy on the other side of the door,
howling like the baby, when he finds
mama's gone. They ain't had long enough
to be together in peace. She never made thirty,
been having babies since thirteen. Got eight of us through,
praise God. Those of us left
cry loud and long, no one has to say
Hush now, don't let them hear you.

I am fifteen, married, learning to aid with birthing,
Granny come, Miss Missy, and I'm taught
no one can save everyone.
We get the child here, my sister,
and all but one step back into the just showing light
of morning. We put mother in the ground,
out in the open, we'll mark her grave and visit.
My body doesn't know yet I'll birth eleven children.
Illness will get many, only seven will survive.
The ones to bury me will bear the biggest burden,
they'll dream of me until they rest; I'll be as heavy as eternity.

With mother's baby wailing, these days she's been alone,
I feel my first child moving in me.
Have they come for each other?
Sewn through us—they want us all—
mother, grandmother, sister. The earth turns over
without much coaxing, men tamp it down,
the box disappearing. Children turn,
in my arms, in my belly. I am here and in between.

Minnie's house in Petersburg and her granddaughters.
The girl in the center of the photo is Shirley, the author's paternal
grandmother, who was delivered in Minnie's bed.

Catching Babies

My mother repeated what my aunt told me, *God brought you here, God made you free*, to every baby. So it sit on my tongue like sugar. Sugar, sugar, sweet home. Sometimes I hear the mothers singing after screaming. Sometimes they are so quiet it scares me. I let them stand and push, hold on to something, hold on to me. Whatever they need. Some come wanting less. I tell them I forget their names, the fathers, bundle peacock flower or cotton root. If my hand must be a guide, I part flesh lovingly. I am gentle as I want folks to be with me. I am listening to God, the trees. How could I know I set those children down and they'd linger beside me? My children restless and wandering away for work, their children under the folds of my skirt. Even birth great grandbabies in my bed almost til the year I die. What is work in this life? Every woman won't survive. Some children still. But I am a comfort to many, some are a world opening to me. I see through their bodies into another life. *You free*, I tell them, *You free*.

Ruddy

1890

Two of my children turn red
in the face when something's

hurt them. Lighter than the others
and everyone knows

they belong to the white man
I used to do housework for.

He had rules. Soon as I could,
I made my way back to the tobacco floor.

Everyone call him Rudd, say my children
look like he spit them out

but when I find Thomas,
smooth as molasses,

kind to my grandmama,
kinder to me, he asks why

I'm not married, I tell him my first husband
died early and now I'm just trying

to care for every bird under my wing.
We make family anyway we can.

He kisses their heads
the same as mine

and every one we raise or make
together, he scolds and holds

in equal measure,
no matter how much dirt

they track in the house, whether they favor us
or have their own face and mind.

Coal miner with his wife and
two children, 1938.

Seems Like We're Building a City

I don't wish it on nobody,
what happened with my son.

Doctor tell us his appendix was bad,
needed an operation

but they're careless, sew him up and leave
the scissors in. Thomas and I

go to everyone who'll listen, one lawyer
take us on and, that boy has troubles

for the rest of his days, but they find
the hospital guilty and settlement comes.

When we get that money, we buy a big plot of land,
make the rows, start setting boundaries

and people come from everywhere.
Every year there is another street

made from us. Another garden.
I fill mine with watermelon, cabbage,

butter beans, my tomatoes so thick
people slice them and add a pinch of salt

each summer. They even come from Pocahontas Island
where them folks been living free

for a hundred years,
but my growing hand, and Thomas's,

turn these acres we had into a bright opening,
something sweet on the tongue.

RIOTING BREAKS OUT AT NORFOLK, VIRGINIA—Six persons were shot during a clash between whites and blacks in the negro sections of the city tonight. Four of the wounded are negroes, of whom two are expected to die.

July 21, 1919

When the soldiers came home
the riots started.

Colored men in uniform
pulled from trains, pushed into streets.

Nearby here, folks thought they'd celebrate a whole week
the men who fought, lost limbs, changed

into equal citizens, but
a punch was thrown,

white policemen emerged
then the Navy, then Marines,

everything turned.
In other places, colored neighborhoods burned

bodies—piled, plum-colored,
plied and picked—became petrified bricks

their eyes: unread books,
each page worn yellow, edges torn.

Medals and teeth
scattered. Here, six shot;

there, some noosed.
O the burning, the tar,

all leveled trees
in the light now,

29

brown smoke, steeple gone,
storefronts missing,

schools and thoroughfares
and porches, given to road and river.

With the heat comes colored men believing
they are worthy of honor

now that they've shown such loyalty—they wear
the brass, name what units they led—

but the mothers know different:
every summer is red.

*the Great Depression was hard to distinguish
when poverty was always a way of life*

1931

Colored folks been broke, Depression ain't made it much worse.

Breadwinners: whole streets of us, whole parishes,

whole neighborhoods—women on the back end of everything running.

Hard-up, struggling. Throwing rent parties, taking in laundry,

in the kitchen making plates or styling hair. Make do however we can.

The polls don't want us, last hired at the factory, but we still

exquisitely made: hair turning back under sweat, dust clinging behind knees

and every dollar our own dollar. We gather at the Old Market

on Saturdays with our wares: what's caught, cleaned and scaled,

cures with herbs and tincture, quilt scraps made into soft

diamonds, north stars—signs for devotion, covering.

Some bought freedom here, now, without having grown wings, we fill the sky.

Every house with heat got a woman's hand in it.

We the industry. We the communion. The engine and offering, the wheels turning.

urg is operated
the principal
horse cars in-
to the suburbs.
one-half miles
nd one-fourth
miles. On the
perated from a
ut the power is
ower or Canal
ck, Old, Syca-
al streets. It
l runs to West

from a connec-
swood Heights,

Old Market House.

The dummy line begins at the western terminus of the electric line and
runs out to the Central Lunatic Asylum, the granite quarries, and to a favorite
summer resort known as "Granite Grove," and also connects with the Norfolk
& Western R. R. about a mile beyond the resort. This line is known as the
Petersburg & Asylum road.

Just beyond its terminus is the village of MATOACA, of 1000 population,
largely employed in the cotton mills there. It is about five miles from Peters-
burg, and it is the intention of the Asylum line to extend to it very soon.

GEORGE BEADLE, a capitalist, formerly of New York, but a resident here
since 1882, owns the franchise for the street railway

Night Class, Peabody High School

1936

They've taught me how to put the alphabet to my name,
been counting for years but never had letters.

Most of the class twice or three times as old as the teachers here.
What will they make of crooked teeth and letters?

They are good and patient children, cleaning the board
filled with our sad chickenscratch. They understand letters

that barely touch. They want so much for us in our dwindling
years. They hold us dear, we're their unplanned letters.

Miss Sue, one teacher, visits the market, buys from my garden, always minds,
says, *You got some stories, Miss Minnie*, tracing freehand letters.

Sometimes we sing, sometimes we sorrow; these brick walls hold
secrets most won't write down. I read headstones now, their stone-clad letters.

They won't take money in exchange for teaching, say *You're owed this and more*.
We thank them by returning, opening our doors; they help address our letters.

The Tenderness of One Woman for Another

There was little play when I was a child.
    I shared secrets with no one,
        had no dress-up clothes or bows.
            I missed other little girls then.

My daughters were my dolls. Spitting up and weary of sleep.
    I was so grateful when the women came,
        took the crying babies from my arms, took my wash,
            scrubbed my kitchen to sparkling.

I could barely lift my head,
    I was so tired, but they
        laid their hands on me.
            We our own assembly.

Passing vittles, counting heads and nickels,
    bragging on children, come by birth or fortune.
        Loving folks' dirt, harboring it, along with light,
            slapping our thighs when the telling gets good.

We are happy to grow old together,
    to cross the changing streets
        to be near each other, though
            our floorboards have worn thin.

They sat watch with me when Thomas was dying.
    After, though the sun was going and they'd worn
        their good shoes, stooped down in the dirt behind the house
            to weed and clear the garden.

In my final years, changed my bedclothes,
    brought willow bark and ginger, said a soft prayer.
        Tied the healing string in knots until the moaning stopped.
            Then took a comb to my hair.

Colored women in town
on Saturday afternoon, 1941.

Perhaps Minnie Sees Mary and Prays for Her Safekeeping

1941

Asylum three miles from here.
Plenty scared of secrets locked inside.
Barely ever bring folks in at night, mostly a police car
with no sirens heading up Washington Avenue
in daylight means a colored child, a girl today,
bobbing wildly, eyes glued to whatever's
flying past the window, trying to figure
where she's headed, cuffed in the back.
She puts me in the mind of my mother,
held and worried long past the crying post.

I am shelling peas on the porch
while everything she knows has turned
into a pot of murky water.
Most sent *up Petersburg*
we'll hear nary a thing about,
unless my granddaughter, a nurse's aid inside
or my grandson, one of the cooks,
thinks there's something worth telling.

I don't know the girl but I hear
they work the women harder than the men.
Sometimes scattered about the yard
weeding or planting in aprons
with no sun hats, bent like I imagine
plenty were in those fields,
like we were in the curing barn, like most
daughters of mine could be, at the hands of
whoever's coming—man or woman, sickly or strong,
with just enough power to shackle them.
Even now, on the radio, the world is threatening war.
With folks here warring on the inside.
Wish they'd fight for my children's children,
the girl passing by, all of us
at the whim of this common danger.

Mostly no one sees the women
until they're brought back
with little to show for their obedience,
their reconstruction, their lost hours.
They might leave with a small sack
of their belongings, sometimes a steady
hand pressed to the land of the living
in one way or another. I rock and hum
as she is carried past every wondering eye.
I raise my hand to her. She sees little,
but I'm holding here, pray she's holding,
maybe string and cord will ferry her
through reef and peril and vine,
I'm hoping she'll come back by me whole,
in a stormless place, an abundant time.

Mary Etta Knight

(1922–2007)

Central Lunatic Asylum for the Colored Insane
Founded in Petersburg, Virginia

1870

Your countrymen have settled a place for you.

We have seen you, beside yourselves,

speaking freely, walking in our paths

and know this insolence

could not be intentional.

Some have wandered

in the mind from birth,

others stumbled upon this sickness

perhaps not at their own hand

—but the land is full of you—

shadows of an old desire.

Denizens, only a cruel god would leave you

without hope, living unregarded,

vagrant, on the street. Here,

we offer a respite and warm bed.

You'll arrive someone else

and, when you go, carry a clear head.

victims killed in 1922 were burned at the stake in a form of torture that most people today associate with the so-called Dark Ages. These horrific acts happened in modern [enter the name of the state where you were born], just a few generations ago. And white people caught the events on film and put the photos in their own family albums

Housed in the years to come
    as whimsy, postcards,
wedding memorabilia,
    in the meticulously kept
albums of school teachers,
    politicians' wives, farmers and passersby,
photos numbered and ordered
    with handwritten notes
that read: *Burning of negro*
    in front of the old City Hall

And coming this year, this moment,
    a girl-child who will be given
many names: beloved, of the sea,
    bitter, mother, grand, patient,
obscene, domestic, nearly gone, wild-
    fire, burden, stripped clean.

What is the aberration? The child or the burning?
    What is a deviation?
Numbering the knick-knacks? Holding the new
    Negro in loving arms?

Behind those captured:
    anniversary horseback rides
at Seven Falls, dinner with friends
    at their new bungalow.
The world aglow with spectacle and modernity.

What they've kept safe
        this bright exposure
will be called everything
        but what it is   *Look, look*
a child will say, pointing

Mary at
seventeen years old.

Mary perfects the Charleston, recalling it for the next eighty years

I was a little bitty thing doing this
laughing, bending

    her knees, her arms crossing each
then up with the legs, high as she can kick

    she snickers and shimmies
Oh yes! she says singing

    Charleston, Charleston
Made in Carolina!

    stretching out the last "I" until
it bends back to her—

    Carolina born and back there
in her mind. She schools us

    about the Geechie dances warming them
many a night near the fire.

    Her Daddy knew a man who built
makeshift radios, a marvel—

    a little church, vaudeville, ball games,
the All-Negro Hour—it was a refuge.

    At four, she rocked her sister.
At eight, she caught her own fish, cooked meals

    on the wood stove.
At twelve, she left school,

    worked in the tilled rows of
field like most.

Had a portrait made at 17,
lied to the preacher about her age

and married a man who sang
in a barbershop quartet.

As soon as they could, set out for Norfolk.
Some called it an old slave port

but they'd buck and wing
with the river of others,

down to Calvary Cemetery,
up to the Lodge,

the channel of folks searching
the glittering city

where the houses were slums
and the children were plenty,

anywhere they landed
better than the toil

they'd left behind but everybody
missed something, someone,

danced for joy, danced for love,
home a dwindling second line.

March 3, 1941

Dear Doll,

Married life is ~~nothing like I thought~~ a different life, for sure. I miss ~~braiding your hair, having plenty to eat~~ you more than I can say. Hope you're in school ~~until the crops come~~. Don't mind ~~them white~~ the other kids yelling from the bus as they pass. Just get all the schooling you can.

We're ~~barely making ends meet~~ doing alright, at least indoors and fed. Sharing a ~~rundown rowhouse in Huntersville~~ modest place with Johnnie's brother and his wife. They're kind to let us ~~pay so many of the bills~~ stay on. I'm almost seven months along. Getting ~~worried~~ big and slow but I still ~~do all the cooking~~ help in the kitchen. Scrub as much as I can too. Not sure what we'll do ~~when we get free~~ after the baby. God'll see us through.

I hope we find our own place soon, but rent is ~~hard to come by when a man spends too much on hooch~~ rising with the war. Everybody wants to live near Church Street ~~though trouble lives there too~~. Harlem of the south they call it. Got ~~ladies of the night, urchins hustling~~ dancing, shops and a trolley that goes for miles, all the Negro business anyone could want. I sent some organdy from the fabric shop. Next time, maybe ribbons, if ~~money holds out~~ you're good.

Found a church with ~~halfway~~ decent folks. They not as flashy as House of Prayer, you know Daddy Grace is there. He parades through town ~~like he some kind of god~~ with women fanning him, them long nails ~~longer than yours, mine or mama's, any woman's~~ shining and an all white suit. I want a quiet kind of spirit myself, like we used to find fishing on the water. I signed up for choir and to help with nursing. That just means I'll ~~hide behind robes and white gloves most Sundays~~ tend to others when they need me to.

Write soon and kiss mama for me. ~~Kiss grandma, too, if she lets you. How's her mind? She still   .~~ Help daddy out whenever you can. I hope you all can come ~~make it seem more like home here~~ see the baby, whatever's in God's plan.

Love,
Sister

June 18, 1941

The clothes are on fire, in her mind,

the clothes are covered in blood.

The spot of lard or flour from cooking spreads

until her clothes are tar and feather.

The clothes are another body, a scaly skin,

an animal covering, a fresh kill.

The clothes are a burlap sack filled

with wet cotton, a factory of tobacco,

a winding sheet. Years later

the clothes will be the evidence

neighbors use, the talk they'll whisper

that children overhear and sing as taunts

That's why your mama's crazy

running through the streets naked

and you just like her   children will say

to her daughters and the fabric will unravel

again and again, like the long night, the lost year,

the still burning mind.

Mary Taken to the Central Lunatic Asylum

She will jump, she says
she no longer cares for the child
after the fire of the mind has taken
her clothes and shoes, her pious tongue,
and thrown them into the street.

The suffering grows in her, settles in her belly like snuff,
and nothing comes as it should:
not a groan or holler, not the doctor on time,
just the child mangling everything, and after,
no blood.   Two stories up, she warns everyone:

The power and the spirit are coming.
And when she gets a hold
of the underside of her husband's
skin, taking it with her over the steep ledge,
with her newborn screaming
in the distance between them,
the siren choir approaching
with its fire and wings,

her husband is dumbstruck,
when they ask if she is herself,
while she curses him, swearing
in a rage, the words coming like spirit,
her fists moving as fast as the mind,
and everyone at arm's length bloodied and weary,

until she is handcuffed and sped away
God willing, she says, to her husband
and something indecipherable
as he signs the large green ledger,
finally reverent, admitting

the god who led him here, who transfigured
and loosed another not unlike herself,
a body outside her body,
coming in another name.

CENTRAL STATE HOSPITAL, PETERSBURG, VIRGINIA
Record of Applications and Admission of Patients for the Month of June 19 41

7

	Names of Applicants	Age	Residence	Correspondence and Postoffice	Application Received	Applicant in Jail or on bail	Epileptic or Feeble-Minded	Habitual Criminal, Etc.	Reviewer or Date Reported	Patient Received at Hospital	REMARKS: Date Will Send for Patient and Other Data
1	Mary Frances Jones	9	Greensville Co	Catherine Jones						June 3	Rtd by Dept
2	Greenlat Preston	74	Rockbridge Co	Emporia Va	June 1 Bail						
3	Emma Kerr	60	Greenmar Co	Dept of Public Welfare	June 3 Bail 3 m					June 6 See letter	Rtd by Welby
4	Irene S. Beckley	32	Roanoke Va	Gordonsville Va	June 5 Jail					June 6	
5	Mary Adele Brown	25	Richmond Va	Roanoke Va	June 10 Jail					June 14	
6	Lula Bell Davis	33	Richmond	City Hall	June 14 Jail					June 16	
7	Fannie Webster	21	Norfolk Va	H.T.P. Boys	June 1 Bail					June 1	Rtd by husband
8	Mary E Carter	20	Gloucester Co	Edward Carter	Vol Bail					June 2	
9	Martha Lewis	29	Fredericksburg Va	Hare Neck Va Jas Lewis	June 3 Bail					June 3	Rtd by Edward Ca
10	Mary Riddick	49	Norfolk Va	328 Walt St Frederick burg Va	June 5 Jail					June 5	Arthur Ba
11	Selena H Burnell	39	Fredericksburg Va	Hattie H Wicks	June 6 Jail					June 6	
12	Annie Belle Clarke	44	Dinwiddie Co	Fredericksburg Va Jerri Clarke	June 7 Bail					June 7	
13	Lelian Virgie Ross	39	Hampton Va	Lucille Ross 325 N Green St	June 9 Jail					June 9	Rtd by Sheriff
14	Georgianne Chambers	27	Buckingham Co	Hampton Va Ruby Hale	June 10 Bail					June 10	Lucille
15	Pearl Eliz Henley	43	Richmond Va	Buckingham Va Sophie Cockerell	June 11 Bail					June 11	Gilbert
16	Virginia Stone	16	Richmond Va	Richmond Va Carry Stone 427 St	June 11 Jail					June 11	
17	Emma Colbert	20	Wythe Co	South Richmond Va Richard Holliday	June 14 Bail					June 14	Rtd by car
18	Laura Bailey Holloway	44	Isle of Wight Co	Wytheville Va Jim Bailey	June 18 Bail					June 21	
19	Nora Davis	40	Richmond Va	Smithfield Va Elizabeth Laura	June 19 Jail					June 20	
20	Queen Elizabeth Hill	38	Richmond Va	922 W Leigh St Richmond Va	June 19 Jail					June 18	
21	Viola Harris	10	Richmond Va	Julia Hill 2710 P St Richmond Va	June 20 Jail					June 21	
22	Elizabeth D Hines	65	Stafford Co	Henrietta Harris 1187 N 31 Richmond	June 21 City Home 3 m					June 26	
23	Mary Bigelow	64	Richmond Va	Zack Hines Brooke Va	June 18 Bail					June 18	Rtd by
24	Margaret Wilson	15	Portsmouth Va	J. L. Bigelow 804 87 James St Richmond Va	June 25 Bail					June 25	L
25	Dorothy Goode	28	Chesterfield Co	Annie + Darnell Wilson 2201 Effingham St	Vol Bail					June 18	Rtd by
26	Mary Knight	19	Norfolk Va	Porter Goode R 7 Co 1 Ettrick Va	June 18 Jail					June 18	
27	Eutha or Eubertha Burnell	26	Richmond Va	John Knight 871 Chestnut ave Norfolk Va	June 18 Jail					June 23	
28	Ellen May Johnson	24	Henrico Co	Wm Burnell 243 Box 63 Richmond Va Robert H Johnson R 7 9 5 Box 375 Richmond Va	Vol Bail June 27 Bail					June 24	Rtd June 24

Ledger for June 18, 1941, from the Central Lunatic Asylum (Central State Hospital) in Petersburg. Mary was signed in on line 26.

MASTER INDEX: CASE RECORD

NAME: **Knight, Mary**   DATE: **June 18, 1941**   RECURRENCE: Visit ✓1 ☐2 ☐3 or more

AGE: **19** (though husband adds a year, perhaps out of fear)   OCCUPATION: **Domestic**

REASON: **Had my first baby June 9th, doctor came late, no afterbirth, no blood, then [profanity]**

CURRENT SYMPTOMS/BEHAVIOR: *Frequent attacks of destructiveness. Seems to [be] aware of approch [sic] of mental storm. Disturbed at intervals. Uses very profane language.*

TO BE COMPLETED: *A survey of the family. It is of the highest importance to have, as fully as possible, a conception of the individual before* [s]*he became afflicted*

COMMITTED AS: **Insane**   PATIENT WATCH: **Suicidal**   DIAGNOSIS: **Manic Dep. Psy.**

IN THE FUTURE WE WILL CALL IT: Postpartum psychosis

COMPLAINTS: **I do not think I have all that belongs to me.**

TREATMENT PLAN: As *resistive behavior from a population considered to be naturally docile and tractable* is cause for alarm, we'll employ a *coercive use of hydrotherapy* such as *the continuous bath, baths of varying temperatures, cold douches, and the wet pack to calm the agitated mind and to control the recalcitrant body. Elements of both treatment and discipline, mechanical and chemical, restraint and seclusion.*

Must show *ability and willingness to work.* To prove her wellness and worth, before release, patient will be employed *making beds, dusting furniture, sweeping floors, work in the laundry, work in the kitchen, work in the dining room.* After she is nearly broken, patient must have, in her right mind and on numerous occasions, *expressed a desire to go home.*

The color blue was full of darkness

From the hallways and branches   sometimes you call

and I never   have the sense   to ask your name.

Sounds like   what my grandmother heard   maybe

before leaving   —stopped cooking   for her children

stopped combing her hair, washing anything—

lived on like this until   she disappeared.

Who are you

to give a woman her mind   or take it

who are you   to carry that power

from one green wall

one steel mirror

to the next   and the next   and

To Calm the Mind

More than twenty years from now when

my last child has been born, I'll remember

the hoses while others despair

at children on the news—

treated like dogs, worse than—

being punished for having

their own free minds.

But all these years before,

they use the water to quiet us.

A hose can peel back skin or curdle it,

cold water begins to burn—

water in the bath that lasts for hours or days,

water sprayed hard as we are lined up against a wall—

until we pass out or shut our mouths.

No one here can stand screaming,

there is little singing. When we get music,

they call it a diversion.

Sometimes my ears are still filled

with what's left.

It's quiet, quiet now.

I have to do something

with my hands.

We are given mops to clear the room.

The water is like an ocean.

Those calling, like the drowned,

gone to the neverending bottom.

Maybe another door will open onto the sea,

if there are doors that can carry the sea,

and they will pass me by.

Every floor can be the briny floor there

or the well I feared all those years

on the land my father farmed.

A child fell inside once

and many nights passed

before anyone thought

to look over its edge.

a fish has broken from the water its rod of a body

A big, pretty fish, my sister-in-law says after she has dreamt it,
translucent and filled with bright copper like fire,
she is sure the child is coming to me and I am filled with worry.

My belly blooms and I am wide as the unpaved walk
along the path leading here, to a place not mine,
a middle place, not borrowed but used, a halfway living.

　　　This is a found baby poem. The child will come despite my fear

and change me for good. The house will be filled with worry for her
even as I am willed away by what she broke (or fixed) in me.
My sleep is restless in the house of no gods, no babies, no husbands

wing-clipped and sick with uselessness. The woman who dreams of my baby
will raise her for the months I'm gone, then fight to keep her.
But when I return, a better brighter more knowledgeable self,

she must concede to the rightful fierce hollow of me,
fish-mother, spirit-rider, woman-wandered brought to something
like hell and back, always with a baby on the brain, to call and quell the lightning.

Building for chronically ill females at the Central Lunatic Asylum (Central State Hospital) in Petersburg.

Two Months and Thirteen Days

(though all her life she believed she stayed for nine months,
long enough to birth another, had she the means)

I return home carrying someone else,
not in my body but in my blood.

       Loss in my body, but in my blood
       nothing's changed. I am just like my mother

something strange, sly and hushed. Why are mothers
every doorway, every host?

       I am every door, give way to every host.
       When you let things in, they haunt or anchor you.

Let children in to haunt or anchor you and
they'll be there forever, long after you've gone.

       When I dream of forever, there's laughter, song.
       I do God's work, with or without him.

God works, with or without me.
I return home burying someone else.

Life's an Ever-turning Wheel

The baby's name is Evelyn, she is the first of seven.
She'll settle me more than the asylum could.
Coming back into the distance, her wonder like leaven
spreading everywhere, taking the place of quiet, like it should.

The years are a spiral. They come with every step:
two boys, four more girls, every one seeking something—
cornhusk dolls, rocks to skip, my lips in their curls.
I clean white women's houses, do what I can, to try to keep them from wandering.

Johnnie is restless, running the streets. He nods
at the bootleggers' house until somebody calls me. I send our boys
to collect him. One follows right behind, picks up his flaws;
the other runs in the opposite direction: preaches hope, knows the Word.

Decades pass, and most forget, as long as the heart stays calm.
I go on living, tend house and home, ignore the blackbirds, read the Psalms.

Clean white homes and smiling black servants
appropriately attired in language and dress

Fix your face
I tell my children

something that's been told to me
when visitors enter.

My tongue, pliable as pie crust
settles soft and silent.

When I am called
I am expected

to end in shadow,
to appear and disappear

like good nature.
Up and back

the broom scurries
as if alive:

my face,
a wretched dance

I follow, as if by will
not need, or biding time, or skill.

Child with toys,
blocks, cook, 1913.

Child with Playthings in Black and White

A small girl is looking for what will fill her hands next.
She holds a porcelain doll tight to her chest.

A tower of lettered and numbered blocks
stacked to her knees. Her eyes drawn to things at her feet—

a mammy doll propped against a low window,
handkerchief on her head, apron sewn to her waist.

a stuffed dog with cloth circles for wide eyes, wired ears
turned toward a figure folding drapery.

On the outskirts of the room, binding a sheet:
brown hands and breasts rise against a well-made crease.

Tweedle Dee, LaVern Baker

1955

I make my own joy
sewing the girls' dresses,
    put the needle between my teeth, spin thread
    around the bobbin, press the pedal to the rhythm on the radio.

Beauty at my hands, like creation
what I dream, I see, comes to be.
    Saturday, sun rising and soon Ms. Terry will knock
    to share the Word. She talks about Jehovah like he's a friend to me.

It's peaceful with the music on,
the children run down the block,
    their voices echo and volley, chorus of mother's hours.
    Given time, I'll embroider flowers, initials in each collar.

I'll make them matching sets, maybe add a row of lace,
I am swaying and bolting fabric in place.
    Nimble and sharp, the pleats are
    near perfect. Nothing's wasted.

I'm happiest when I can hold
my gifts. I count it as grace to dance,
    roll my hips. Johnnie takes the back steps
    and finds me singing.

He spins me around the room til we are dizzy,
til the oven timer buzzes, til another song plays.
    Laughing, ears ringing, I iron the dresses,
    careful of everything I've made.

Southside mother sewing
with children, 1955.

The Negro Travelers' Green Book, 1957

Last baby born this year

    something green come from heaven

say all the folks who say Amen

    There are many legends the old people will recall to you

Baby born Black and Green Book says

    Assured protection for the Negro Traveler

last passage this year

    through the negro traveler

Now we are passing the savings on to you

    the womb is a road bruised black and red

The tense world affairs still smolder

    and our Green Book says

To see and learn how people live

    Last daughter sees, her mama learns

The White traveler has no difficulty

    in want of rest, in need of peace

Where and how to go . . . where to stop

    Seven children born Black

Until the fear of war eases, we trust you will use your discretion

    seven is heaven's number, six is the Devil's

and this daughter is the last knot

    in the rope, knot of the tree

green and black, and read, gift of God's

    People   an opportunity

"Daddy" Grace's Fourth of July Parade
in Norfolk, 1958.

remains of the stained glass windows of the 16th Street Baptist Church

The Kingdom Hall is small. There are no stained glass windows
but when those girls are killed in Birmingham, we are still afraid.

A bomb, they say, somebody in the town hid it on church grounds
before Youth Day. Set it for the children.

They'll kill anybody, for anything—a little boy with a limp,
freedom fighters, soldiers, presidents. Even come to God's house

when it's convenient. Hate is like the shards of glass: pieces stuck
everywhere, for years, some skin might shed it on its own

but the rest will burrow in. All winter, we look over our shoulder. All decade. All century.
They'll kill Malcolm. They'll kill King. They'll kill another Kennedy.

A drunk white man jumps the curb and kills my mother,
holding her granddaughter's hand. That child will walk fine

but never recover. None of our daughters will understand. We'll return
to supplication, while some overreach God with their demands.

We only preach, we don't march. We'll clean the rubble
and lay many questions at the altar.

Where does your kindness end? we ask our neighbors.
They think we're a nuisance, at their doors again with Bibles in our hands.

Rainy Night in Georgia, Brook Benton

1970

Spring and even the youngest sprouting now, smelling herself, almost to junior high
and those boys walking past the house trying to get a glimpse of every one I got.

The oldest, already running after a pretty man, but nothing's all roses.
I don't pretend being in love won't wear you out.

Even on the radio they know what it feels like:
like being caught in a downpour with nowhere to run.

The problem is: we all long to hear it.
Voice just as smooth, Brook ain't lost a step.

I turn it up, easing the broom beneath the stove, trying to keep out
the dirt that always settles around my door. His voice dips low on *heavy*

and whoever's playing the bass strums the notes
just after his sorrow like a begging man coming back for more.

When Johnnie went to France, fighting Hitler, he says he held my picture
like Brook does in the rain. Soon one daughter will write her beau,

and he'll hold their picture tight in Vietnam. The storms never stop,
I try to tell them but love is a lonely binding thing.

I read in a magazine the song was written about Marietta, Georgia.
I'm tickled at that. Maybe I loved it because it came after my name,

loved me back. Deep underneath it, there I was, there were all the girls
hoping someone was pining after their image,

the whole world covered with them—
lovers in the rain, restless, the sky, a reminder:

no matter where you run, home is beckoning,
a woman sweeping the kitchen waits.

Mary's daughter Shirley
and her beau, Bobby.

Ars Poetica #214

My mother's mother had seven children, she was named after Mary, no angel appeared. I always loved the misshapen vessel, the glass bowl on her table that held messages and pretend fruit. God wanders into the living room and changes the shade. Aren't the stars more plentiful than us and named? Her children were so loud, I heard them coming, my mother was the last. They crowded any house, weren't allowed to sit in windows during storms. All the families on the street respected fury. Their bedrooms, flights of stairs, attics, basements and lawns, filled with idols. A firm hand might cure you or end you in another time. Her children were a cauldron. She was a quiet song. They flew under a bridge near dusk; she lost count of them and gathered heavy, shiny things. The carapace on the table, fragile but laden as iron. It could have been her mirror; the children passed it with little regard. How does one make so many unlike herself? What did she hear—newborns, ghosts, birds of prey—what were the terms of the long silence of reimagining? Always in an apron, her quilts pressed and gleaming, even after the grandchildren, one by one by one, took up space on her bed. Our little hands smudging the looking glass we weren't supposed to touch, our summer heat packing the back room. She never seemed to tire of us, our salty sweat, oak and ocean air, never raised her voice. We were part of the land, had a hand in the sky turning, the bulbs underground, lying dormant then. Only once, after that first child, did she lose her whole mind, though by the winter I came, it waned at times. I imagine my grandfather dumbfounded, as I was at seventeen, by the calm woman coming undone, complaining about the thick swell of birdseed covering the floor. *Sweep it up*, she'd say louder and louder, *Can't you see it?* And I'd sweep until my mother came and took the broom from my hands. *There's nothing there*, she'd remind her mother. *Don't humor her*, she'd scold me, *How could that help anyone?* A bridge bearing us both, reminding us to mind the dark, the light, whatever was there. What we gathered was only half right, so much of the floor was bare.

The Two White Women I Cleaned For Send Checks
Until The Day I Die Or Until They Do, Whichever Comes First

It could be devotion.

It could be guilt, maybe kindness.

We die together, always wondering what

we missed in each other: was I a comfort?

Were they a holding place, a pen?

Writing letters solves little of the mystery,

a reminder we live, wound

around each other, conductors passing back and forth

what brightness we could hold.

The world was heavy and hard. You loved

my work, every day. I rose, I returned.

      *

My work: every day I rose, I returned.

The world was heavy and hard. You loved

what brightness we could hold

around each other, conductors passing back and forth.

A reminder we live, wound.

Writing letters solves little of the mystery,

were they holding a place, a pen

we missed in each other? Was I a comfort?

We die together always, wondering what

it could be—guilt, maybe kindness?

It could be devotion.

Mary Admires James Brown's Casket

Pure gold. Ain't never seen nothing like it. Clean.
Y'all put me away like that, horses and all.

My aunts, my cousins, my mother and I, laugh and laugh and laugh
in the nursing home. *And where the money coming from?* I ask.

She looks stern at me, *All that education,*
you got plenty money.

But this is false hope. I have student loans,
I have dreams, I will have debt forever.

She raised seven children, had a husband cancer killed thirty years before.
No pension, no land, no inheritance. We're stuck where we are.

I hate to tell her. *James don't know what kind of casket he's in,*
I say instead, as we watch his carriage pass the Apollo.

But everybody know he was something special, she says,
the throngs of brown hands reaching

to touch what's left of a complicated life.
We will dress her in flowers and ivory

not one month later; I'll find her pearls and matching shoes.
My cousin will curl her hair, color her lips. We will spend

too much money for the steel blue casket. My mother will go
as far as the graveside until she collapses. If the world isn't

mourning, we surely won't know it. At the repast, we'll play
It's a Man's Man's Man's World. Everyone will shake their heads

and sing the chorus. People come from everywhere,
the house is overflowing, *She was really something,*

they'll say. *Y'all put her away real nice, looked just like herself.*
No one calls her The Help.

Most of the night, no one's studying me,
I stay in the kitchen—clean every dish, kiss every cheek,

sweep the crumbs, wipe down the counters—work to keep
the living going in our growing, weary hours.

There is going to be a resurrection of both the righteous and unrighteous

I'm poor and near twilight, a blue hour
Some white folks see me; some Black folks hold me
Every place I've been, we're tethered

In the large army of women
Blood but different
Each a crest and current, infinite

Grandmother went mad
Her mother wasn't free
Bondage is abundant, it colors us

My daughters, my daughters
They love and cut up and worry
I anchor them; we stay in stitches, we falter

God is in the wreckage
God is the water, the oars, the lighthouse
I preach to everyone I can

I hold God in me
I hold light and lightning
I'm a rod, a conductor, I'm devoted

Long after I die
There will still be crying
The land is no sanctuary

I am like most mothers
I color all the corners—
I'm coming back, be ready

What We Had to Pass Through to Get Here

Commemorative Headdress For Her Journey Beyond Heaven

1830

I sat the early night under watchful care of guardswomen—Lilly (who wants to be Dawn), her small girl Rose (who will become Iona) and Eve (who will stay Eve in this life, one eye a weary cloud and one on my unveiled head)—all huddled in our dirt quarters, waiting to be discovered. The night cut from both ends gave us little time for breathing, less for tracing the route in my hair. They use wool card, water and seed oil to fashion a plat. Plotting the straight and winding way, a comb made from bits of bone burns my scalp. Eve sees the route, sometimes with her good eye closed, and I was born brave—surly and wry white folks say, meaning: I must be watched for all my wandering into the wrong row, the lash, anywhere almost a country, a reckoning of its own. I am almost born a bird, say these women who saw me landed here, almost a comet—wild-eyed, strands streaked with gray, face ageless. I leave tonight with all the makings of an unknown journey. I run for a doorway, river, hearth, cave with a ladder. If I am caught, what body will return? My crown, they'll loose me of it. If I am dragged back, they'll burn lie into my skin. In heaven, I'll have my body. Wade past what freedom they know. This furrow of want and the root in my hair—the patience of the wild—guiding me. The guards make me repeat what comes before the map: trace black moss along swamp's edge, find the stone mile post at the base of the water where dying trees bend and lean. Sabbath Eve. Nothing on the path but stands of angels, also hiding, before the deep tract of living. Scarf perfectly black as skin and thin to keep the map from unraveling. Years from now, remembering this, it will seem like a dream—brief sleep in the hollow of a tree, my palm: a lover reading my hair.

Eden Before the Fall: Southern Pastoral

Something like paradise
The old myths say

The endless hills
Green and steady as envy

Clay roads paved with dawn
Red like flesh undone

The tree of life was ecstatic, weeping
Angels weren't yet at the door

But everywhere the animals were called
By their given names

Jane and George, Miss Anne and Master
Hope and *Desire* they called the ships

No one could pass through
Without permission

The houses were grand
The columns appeared

As if by providence
Out of thin air

White Children and the Intimate Landscape of Defeat

After the War, the little lost inherit the broken land,

    harvestwork, the heavy plow and cutlery,

    the precision skill demands.

The men are in pieces, just like the trees: hairy, hewn, wild

    maybe white? maybe Black?

    scorched inbetween.

Left to mothers without inheritance or apron-strings,

    this strange poverty:

    nothing saved. The dead unhidden,

dogs taking bodies, hogs, anything at hand.

    There is no pain like uncertainty,

    the belly reminds you.

None of the freed children

    look like children—their faces worn

    with a delicate flash.

Everything still burning. The tracks torn

    and bent like ribbon. Forests laid to waste—

    so little to be seen in the underlight of squalor.

Who could I be? the scolded

    ask mirrors and ballots and fewer

    fathers who've returned.

This shifting in the blood—unnatural, soundless.

    My hands are clean, the children plead,

    why should they be stained?

The black mammy, like the southern lady,
was also born in the white mind

Spook or angel, the flimsy mixture

minced and force-fed:

mangled imagining.

One, a porcelain delicacy;

the other, also impossibility—

unsexed, hexed, invisible and looming.

The men who'll sweep

and dervish them, fixed

to their breasts and beds,

will be treasures to the women:

what they'll birth, unearth,

appraise, or miscarry.

O invention, O futility, how you'll hold

each other, how you'll swing,

how you'll tarry.

25 days after I am born

a man is killed in Mobile, Alabama. It is 1981, nearest what some will call the last lynching in America. *The business of our nation goes forward*—a star leads and hostages are freed while Michael Donald walks from the corner store. He is 19, the youngest of six, a college boy. He will miss class the next morning and Sunday dinner; he will not bring the cigarettes to his sister. Those weeks after spiriting me into the world, my mother watches the news, looks over at my father too frequently, calls his name each time he heads to another room—delirious in her exhaustion and fear—where was he, would he disappear? And the little girl, what world was this for her to enter? Crosses burning on the county courthouse lawn, then other sons with ropes and guns, looking for anyone, find Michael Donald walking, ask him for directions, a sign for old haints. They show him the rifle and what can he do but be forced into the car, driven past this life into the next. Years later, in an unimaginable victory, his mother will bankrupt the KKK, demanding they pay for her loss and others, while my mother, like so many, carries me daily to school around the corner, insists on watching until I am beyond the large blue doors. Mothers are God again, and they will not go quietly; they know everything born will need to be fed, even children hung from low branches in their jean jackets and muddy tennis shoes, carried out of the wood into the light of everyone's suffering.

Author and her parents, Mary's daughter Doris
and her husband Robert.

because the scale of our breathing is planetary, at the very least

There is a way for humans to learn from each other
                              I won't lie: it does involve pain

*if the scale of breathing is collective, beyond species and
sentience, so is the impact of drowning*

so we'll have to sit with our embarrassment and evolution,
      our altered, long-carried, waterlogged skin

*

We have figured out how to map the billions of genomes,
      how to change colors of flowers and count forests on the ocean floor,
but equations can't tell us everything

                You've come to fear me more from
the not knowing, the knottiness all around me

              You know nothing of
the depth of my grief, and the leagues of my love

How can something so far be so bright?
               I know it seems I've dreamed this
                   but my grandmothers are with me as sure as there is light

*

Time is absolute, space is not—we will agree on when we arrived
      but how far we've traveled is a trick of the mind

              You may see it differently, the axis of symmetry—
how fluid is the weight of history? How quickly you can fling it
      from your shoulders like excess water or a showman's cape

*

Everything—pulsars, bad decisions, tradition—wants to live

We hate to admit when we've caused harm, when we need stitches
    but this is existence: everyone, all at once, refusing

    to determine how we might name betrayal
and who will be the animals carrying us back
    to the sites of disappearance, the irontraps with teeth, the broken reef

                *

Where I'm from "see" means to follow with the eyes
and "I see you" means I will not erase you

    the same sound "sea" means
            every place that passes between us
        "caught between the devil and the deep blue sea"
means you can't escape what's left for you

        or some walked into the ocean—should I forgive you for this?

                *

I do want the planet to mourn us
            I do want to bend the arrows of time
    I do want every atom, every animal, to love the women who have loved me:

    allow me this selfishness
and I'll work on seeing a creature for what it is, what it could be—

    everything that thrives runs on the rhythm of water
        held by the moon,

the invisible string bearing the weight of satellites, everyone of us raised
    on appetite, craving, mother-light

The Domestic who is the Bearer of the Present

The hungers who birthed me

wait to be resurrected,

come back famished in dreams.

They leap and dance, call for water,

warble on with insistence,

skin my back, skin my knees.

There is no outgrowing them:

faces like petals, fingers like vines,

hair full with silken wool, mouths like waiting fruit.

Everything we bury comes back again

or we grieve the upturned plot

and count it ruined.

O faithful slave, what am I becoming?

You are a tender whip, wound in me.

You push into my side with your insatiable

demands: *Bring us back. Say we lived.*

If God couldn't keep you, who can?

O, burdened living

riveted and riven by the dead,

love is a debt we must repay.

Call out to them if you are worn sick:

O Master, O Maker, aren't you

finished yet?

The *Lose Your Mother* Suite

Unlike my grandparents, I thought the past was a country to which I could return

They knew better. Going back was like   A wound opening,
salting broken skin, resetting bones.   chasing some (impossible? American?) dream,

As a child, I insisted on   playing in the dirt. Drumming up
time like a hanging tooth.   the body, unanchored; the bite, a sharp misery.

1859 was a world away, the curator said.   The roads there were yellowing.
The sky was haint blue.   Work was given to children or machines.

One of my grandmothers was born then,   I said, *She would have known plenty, even at six*,
the curator assured me *about slavery*.   I asked, *What did the War mean for children?*

Lots of missing trees, famine, wandering—   what most would try to erase from memory,
clearing land begins with execution.   not carrying out but killing the thing.

Given time, my grandmothers knew: Grew orchards, hemlines, houses
stitching a body was a gruesome thing.   and still left us here to wean,

I scour the maps of unfamiliar harbors,   a wide open space, wondering,
what will love demand forever?   what can we make clean?

II.   *tumbling the barricade between then and now*

Cousins come whenever love demands we clean house.
Things gathering dust become our dowry:

porcelain cowries, upturned tusks, one pearl
earring and clown-faced figurines—

we find them scouring grandmother's closets and floor.
Trinkets left to us harboring burdens on earth.

What could she have kept to appease us—notes? luck?
Barely anything short of her coming back would relieve us.

We sweep the crumbs of adornment into a pile,
near the threshold, beside our faith,

our heavy laughter, our misery.
All gone, she taught us when we begged for milk

or stories of her mother. Now we bear children
and their undoing.

Little things we possess,
left here in ruins.

III. *liberating my grandmother . . . from the small, small world*

Left here in ruins, I'll believe any yarn someone's woven is fact:
      History would call her a sharecropper, I say, *So she was destitute? Poor?*

She was fat, my father's mother scolds me, *loved to eat. Had plenty.*
      Could figure money down to the penny and grow anything.

Minnie, her great-grandmother, is no figment for her
      just as she, my grandmother, is a vessel for me.

Grandmothers are small planets;
      granddaughters, moons or rings. Something

orbiting. Tenuous at best but fixed.
      We think we know too much, but

they keep us straight, are the living proof.
      Tell it right, my grandmother says. She, the girl

holding Minnie's faint edges,
      the girl holding the girl holding me.

IV.   *it has always been difficult for me to hold my tongue*

The girl scolding me   was usually   my mother
but she couldn't bridle everything.   Her mother, Mary

would laugh at my tactlessness.   I'd say anything
to anyone   without fear.

I told her where   babies came from
once while she was hanging   clothes on the line

though she hadn't asked.   I wonder what she thought
of my generation   the almost nation

of us   crowding her yard and living-
room   telling what truth we knew

any way we liked to   even about bodies, even
to nurses and men.   How strange I must have been

a new citizen   armed with disregard
or was I   the world changing   daughter come apart?

V.   *everyone had grown weary of me*

Was I the world? Strange daughter—some part
inexplicable bursting, riot,
Orion or sound being born?

Eyelet fashioned by swollen hands, an art,
perhaps, a star, some core? Everyone tires
of looking at what no one can explain.

One speck in the universe starts the world again.
When we are born, we offer nothing
and so much is required.

I wish I could say there was joy but
my mother was the speck The Help grew,
the spare world kept inside secretly

while work was calling, a kick in the gut.
Nothing was easy. In another dimension,
someone already holds

pieces of us, asking
Whose mess is this?
sullying everything.

VI. *across the surface of my studied speech*

Mess like this sullies everything:

> my grandmother will call and say *Who's that white lady*
> *on your answering machine?*

She will laugh and I will wonder what's missing?

> (What did I forget? What does it mean
> to lose your mother? Am I brilliant yet?)

Pretty-mouthed girl with perfect diction.

> How my teachers praised me. Didn't they love
> my lost convention, were they equipped to raise me?

If you lose your mother, tongue,

> are you a new beginning? Will the
> breaking be for love or will you hate

whatever's ending? Going back might kill you,

> progress is a blacklist. Your voice:
> an afterlife, shadow, fist.

Exhibit at the Smithsonian's National Museum
of African American History and Culture,
with the author in shadow in the doorway.

VII. *I was born in another country*

An afterlife, shadow, gift: my grandson is on the phone
    singing some song he's made into my husband's ear.

He is born and the world changes;
    we're in another country again.

It's coming for you: time.
    Soon someone will call you grandmother,

someone will expect you to have answers, to slide them
    a few dollars from that hidden billfold, to make the greens.

We're bound by what we make here. One hundred years ago, this was a different place.
    Two hundred years ago, we would have called who we could family.

The child would have belonged to no one, really. The mangled cord
    of history wears us all out: the epochs they lived without want of me,

the time before I was loud and needed here. Family is more than blood,
    more than proximity. *God, where you been?* we ask of the newly living.

VIII. *my unruly tufts twisted into two French braids*

God, where you been? we ask the wide-toothed comb,
the hands parting hair. Strands gracing the blades and ground,
swept into a mound of memory, then burned
or bound. I was a bald-headed baby.
But the women prayed for me. Mother
bought soft brushes til one curl turned
to streaming plaits, the rows trimmed with foil
and marbled beads, the braids lush and greased.
Many days I came home wild—style lost
to wind and whirring. Always clumsy,
always dirty. I am an only child.
I'm sure my mother worried—what ruin
would entangle me, what couldn't she gather
and undo? What on earth would straightening prove?

IX.   *a blend of peoples and nations and masters and slaves*

What does straightening prove? It's all crooked.
There is no metaphor here.
Everything's something someone's said
on their knees, a prayerbook
for the awfully sorry or spectacles,
a handmade pleading.
God bless the sick in the head,
the unchained, wanderers
and those stuck at the whipping post.
Just one kind of folks,
really: ghosts. All of us
sewn into the hem or row,
hair or gait of another.
As sure as you are living,
someone worries when
you'll leave the earth.
Some mother cried at your birth in
love, or grief or fury. These hands
I'm laying now
dream you a country
meant to harbor whatever's coming
and has passed.
Who could imagine
the crisscrossed path,
the rapture and garble
that makes you, makes me?

X.   *say your name softly . . . people will think*
     you are pleading for help

Who could imagine the crisscrossed path, the women who make me
a winding road. Yellow-brick or dirt-slick, who am I not tending?

I'll cast off the men for another time. They'll come to glory
after their mothers, their wives, all birth and bellies fraught, tending.

We beg for nothing. Eat starch. Crave dirt. Make a way.
God's desire, his wet and writhing dream. Pomegranate, apricot, unending.

If the house belongs to someone else, land isn't ours, no talents,
no silk, are we godly? Sun up to sun down, the whole lot tending.

Even if he raise his hand, nobody break you but you. Say *You didn't give me*
nothing I can't take with me. He'll look stone-faced, but he'll be pretending.

Our names became outlandish—we were making what we longed for—
called the girlchild *Everything Imagined*, built a vine, crop tending.

When the seasons have dwindled, I'll call to myself *Remica? Remica?*
scared my mind will have turned on me, strayed, stopped tending.

XI. *the more ground covered, the more liberated you became*

I am scared my mind will turn on me.
I am scared I will be naked in a burning
house. I am scared my children won't outpace me.
I am scared my children (who aren't made by me)
believe I am a sad imitation of the others.
I am scared I will gather in a room
where everyone will ask me to remember
and when I don't lie they'll say *I'd hate to be you.*
I've lived long enough to be scared my kidneys
will give out on me. I've lived long enough to know just
when they should. I have never shared my fears
with anyone; I am scared they will map the land
and take liberties. Will the women be ashamed?
I'm scared to ask. What will live again? What will die with me?

XII.   *Diaspora was really just a euphemism for stranger*

What will die with me? What will live again?
I am a dispersion in all the kingdoms

of the earth. There is no holy silence
in my version of America—the cut from under,

stolen over, barnacle and invention. I am called
Black here and elsewhere but mostly known as

strange. All of the women I am dragging to the surface
perhaps against their will, to kill and kill but name,

who of them will find anything like home,
what's beyond the slave? Not tobacco fields,

not Africa, all an incomplete heaven.
Everyone dreams of being wanted,

always the leaven worrying the sieve. God,
when are the women allowed to grieve?

XIII. *fragments of stories and names that repeated themselves*

When are the women allowed to grieve?
They plunge their hands into the bodies
of others, bringing children to light.

Over and over, they salvage blood
in their beds, the fragments multiplying,
as the living choose names honoring the dead.

Some born still and, still all the rest given
to earth's greedy hands by way of time or fear,
lack or worry, flag or Black tax.

Nikky Finney says *The grandmothers were right
about everything*. They don't forget
the language of disaster.

Sometimes their sons come from battle, to run
from mobs ready with fire. The women who sacrificed
say it plain: *Love brought you home, but it sure do make you tired.*

XIV. *Nostalgia or regret could kill you in a place like America*

Love brings you home, wears you out, makes you tired on the inside. You ask yourself who you might have been in another time. But in truth, in any America, no one would care for you like they should. You'd still be making your own joy every way you could—wearing velvet, singing loud, kissing the fat on a baby's thigh, feeding whoever's hungry. All the women before you, a tapestry you wish you'd held, lives you wish you'd seen. But they'd tell you *You can't be with everything*. The further you dig the more it haunts you, every life, a slow drag, they knew, going back was like a wound opening.

XV.

Going back was like a wound opening.
    What can we make clean

left here in ruins,
    holding the girl holding me?

Was I the world changing, daughter come apart?
    (Mess like this sullies everything.)

An afterlife, shadow, fist:
    God, where you been?

What on earth would straightening prove,
    the crisscrossed path, the rapture and garble that makes you, makes me?

I am scared my mind will turn on me.
    (What will die with me? What will live again?)

When are the women allowed to grieve?
    Love brings you home but it sure do make you tired.

XVI. Saidiya's Cento

Everyone had grown weary of me,
my unruly tufts twisted into two French braids
tumbling the barricade between then and now,
a blend of peoples and nations and masters and slaves.

The more ground covered, the more liberated you became:
fragments of stories and names that repeated themselves
across the surface of my studied speech
liberating my grandmother . . . from the small, small world.

Say your name softly . . . people will think you are pleading for help.
It has always been difficult for me to hold my tongue.
Unlike my grandparents, I thought the past was a country to which I could return.

I was born in another country—
diaspora was really just a euphemism for stranger.
Nostalgia or regret could kill you in a place like America.

What Survived

Minnie and Mary Live to 84

Born slave,   Born free,

my heart gave out,   my kidneys

failed and betrayed me.   won't filter out

Too big maybe, delivered   what they need.

what little love   The world had

kept me alive.   the soft carapace of the body

Dark and wondrous,   steady as steel

my hands are skillful,   until I become

a slave again   a bent flower, heavy stone.

even in my people's eyes   But sun, a new day, comes

when they ask   over and over,

all those questions.   worry won't have me.

I run to the fishing hole,   I work the garden,

sing in the light.   pray in the dark.

I believe the past is one teacher,   The body withers,

not the whole spirit.   not the whole mind.

Where did you come from / how did you arrive?

I ripped my mother being born

    and I am the only.

        The oldest ripped my grandmother

            and still came more.

We have a family history

    of losing our heads,

        of no one listening,

            of telling someone before.

We are raucous and willful,

    loud as thunder.

        No one can forget us,

            we bear our teeth.

We pass through bodies

    like summer heat. We eat

        and thicken, worry men.

            They plead and suffer, come again.

I entered the world

    a turning storm,

        but no one stopped me

            though they'd been warned.

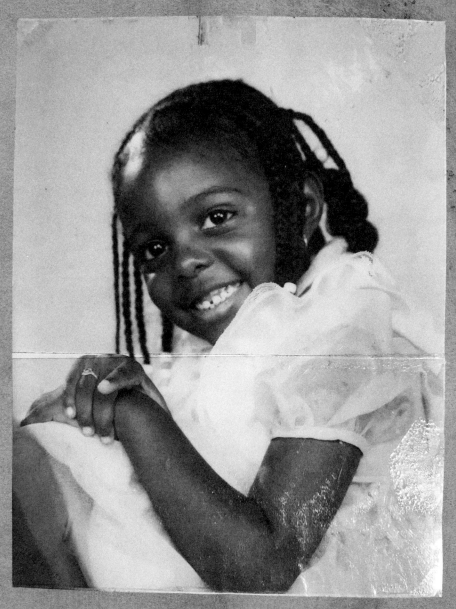

The author at four years old.

There Is Nothing In Your Story
That Says You Should Be Here

Let's just call it what it is: miraculous

    or nothing but time and chance,
a hair's breadth of the Divine sense of humor,

    what wasn't planned
but tickled everyone watching:

    first, the nearly indestructible forced onto ships
then babies born on plantations, surviving the South,

    daughters and sons—impatient and fearless—
heading North: a girl follows her sister from Norfolk

    to Fort Monmouth, a boy sees her picture on a mantle
and vows to marry her. His father fell in love with a waitress in Petersburg

    who served him sweet potato pie and milk,
a baby herself, and he slick-sleeved,

    just stationed at Fort Lee. He carried her
as far from there as he could, on and on this love

    up the coast, in the heart of all wars,
children die and children gather, one finds another

    and every star extends its hand to a new windswept door.
There should be no possibility of you

    but here you are: an opening, a crossing.

And here, every instrument brimming with sound
    every seed a body, inconspicuous in the garden.

You are a spectacular disruption, a tempest—
    and with that knowledge

that you have been remarkably made,
    call to yourself in the distance:

The world will arrive to meet you
    and you will not be afraid

In My Best Dreams They Are On The Water

In the quiet, on your own,
nothing can touch you.

You listen to rustling of leaves, the constant song of redbirds and jays,
the concert orchestrated beneath you.

Breathing at the surface, small things
unseen, create the ripples and circles, but let you be.

As you are patient and skillful, you've made a lure and cast it carefully,
a pretty fish—a shining, writhing wonder—will appear.

If it is willful, you'll bear down and hold the line. Your arms, full of power,
used to carrying jars of lard, bags of flour, children, well and unwell,

even grown others, who must be lifted
into a bed, an afterlife.

The fish gather near the eddies, around fallen trees, a respite
from the weight of water. In my dreams, you are still someone's daughter,

she calls to you eventually. When you leave the river and enter
the house, children are grateful you've arrived. They are alive

and will be well fed. You gut the fish, remove its scales.
Dip it in buttermilk and cornmeal, fry it in hot grease.

There is strawberry pie and cola. Every plate is full.
Ain't no politician save you; ain't no man make or break you.

You are here and every bounty.
I hope you rest. I'll wait at the edge.

I'll pray for low tide and abundance. When you come
you'll show me how to let the stillness into my body, to grow into myself—

what to throw back into the everlasting,
when to lift my skirt and splash onto the shore,

when to mix salt with salt and sun with sun, when to become
another part of the earth, hungerless, a corridor.

Refusing Rilke's *You must change your life*

6,000 books and counting. Large seashells
in plastic bins collected by your daughter.
A wooden spoon laced
in scripture. Anniversary cards
for old loves, cards for housewarming,
for gratitude, one ivory program
with raised lettering. Ceramic
dishes older than you
carried from your mother's house,
her mother's house, whoever
made them useful first. Unlaced shoes,
beltless jackets, strapless gowns
and satin robes. A wooden chest carved
by hand telling a story not unlike
the years of photos kept inside.
Old concert leaflets, dental records,
things you've been searching for
and have misplaced—certificates,
ironclad agreements, signatures
that might save some if others
are hampered by death or waste.
A glasswork brooch painted over,
a safe deposit box with no key
or lock, a pair of baby socks
and toys full of dust, a statuette—
Black bride and groom—above
the dresser filled to the brim with us.

*I am trying to carve out a world where people
are not the sum total of their disaster*

But for the grace of God
one might begin and
this must be the life of a woman.

I will barely touch the surface
of all it took to keep them here.

They taught us to nod to others in the street,
to holler love, to knead eggs and butter and flour
into yeast rolls larger than fists, to coax and heed the land.

Looking at us, every god
must be astonished and envious—

what could leave us finished?
Grandmother's grandmother,
enslaved by someone's daughter,

enslaved and someone's daughter, held
her mother out to us with eager, capable hands.

What couldn't she grow, what couldn't she stand?
And the man beside her, kissing her neck at night
before being thrown into war in the nation and abroad,

barreled back to her, her creases, her starch
and hand-me-down pots, her thick hair and threadbare dresses,

loved every falling-apart piece of her
down to the rocked-over heels on her shoes.
Every lie told says there was no love

between them but everywhere
I turned, here it was:

slow drags, belly laughs;
few reckon with their joy.
Most will make happiness a footnote

along with evenings on the porch,
hitting the number straight or box,

motherwit, innerlight.
O glory and genius
of unfathomable invention:

to raise overfull children
with a guiding soft hand.

Strange how everything can become
a symbol—a cushaw gourd,
songs sung to trees, hair luster, dreams—

any charm one carries can be
a hopeful, treasured thing.

They helped us find bottles
with corners of homespun shine
and place our lips above the hollow

until they sang. They were not angels,
they were not myth. They saved

pennies and baby hair and wedding rings,
grew big as a pianobox, broke through fever.
Their suffering wasn't everything.

Room Swept Home

Mama say, *Jah holy. House holy. Both clean.*
Keep things in their places. Is disorder ever clean?

Preserve the skin alive by soaking,
bathe and lather high end low, clean.

This water in the Chesapeake, the Bay
bodyfull and green. All tide swept by heavy row: clean.

The needle's eye and day's work both seamless:
hem and stitching, knife-edge sharp, sewn clean.

Gristle bone sucked and crushed—teeth
mincing meat to red marrow—clean.

Sweep porch steps, no steps, dirt path—pristine;
any small patch of earth we're given: Godstruck, bare, but so clean.

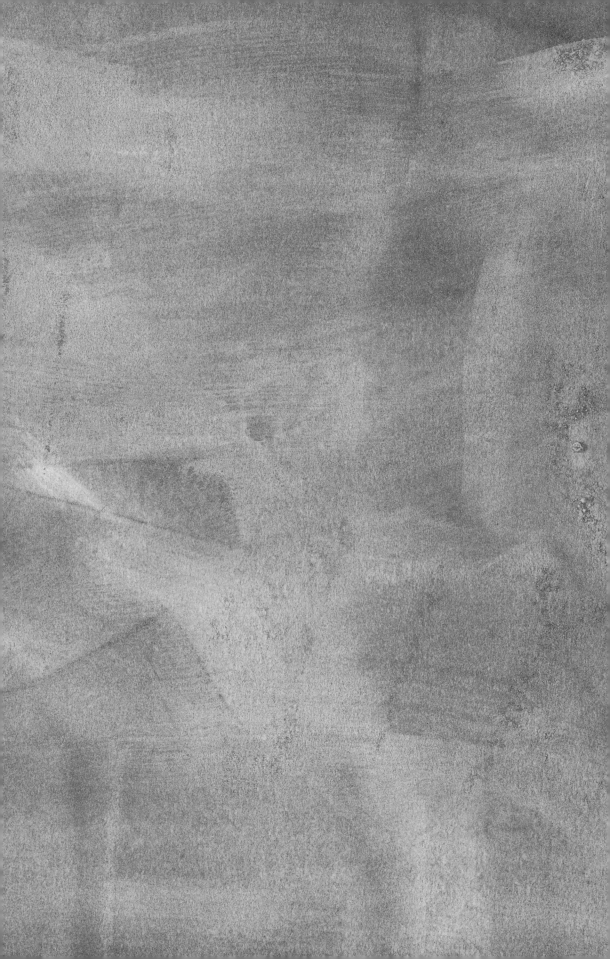

Acknowledgments

Grateful acknowledgment is given to the following publications where some of these pieces first appeared (or will appear), sometimes in different versions or under different titles: "In the Corridor, "Lost Friends," and "Commemorative Headdress For Her Journey Beyond Heaven," in *Common-Place*; "*The Domestic who is the Bearer of the Present*," in *Transition Magazine*; "*Where did you come from/how did you arrive?*" and "The *Lose Your Mother* Suite," sonnet VI ("*across the surface of my studied speech*"), on Poem-a-Day, Academy of American Poets; "The Negro Travelers' Green Book, 1957," in *Black Bone: 25 Years of the Affrilachian Poets Anthology*; and "Wanderlust," in *Won't You Celebrate With Me: An Anthology of Contemporary Black Poets*. "Mary Taken to The Central Lunatic Asylum" was a finalist for the Graybeal-Gowen Prize, and was then published by *Shenandoah*.

All thanks belongs to Jehovah God who inspired 1 Cor. 1:27–29, which reminds us that ". . . *God chose the foolish things of the world to put the wise men to shame; and God chose the weak things of the world to put the strong things to shame; and God chose the insignificant things of the world and the things looked down on, the things that are not, to bring to nothing the things that are, so that no one might boast in the sight of God.*"

Thanks to Gregg Kimball at the Library of Virginia, whose work on Susie R. C. Byrd and the WPA Project helped inform my own searching.

And to the entire Library of Virginia team of librarians and archivists, without whom much of my searching for the context of life in Petersburg, Virginia, as well as for Central State Hospital records, would have been futile. I owe a great debt to Virginia State University librarians and archivists as well.

To Lucinda Rush Wittkower, Karen Vaughan, Steven Bookman, and other Old Dominion University librarians who were always ready to try to answer the most intricate questions.

To Cynthia Lynne Harrison, my forever librarian, and all librarians at Norfolk State University.

To librarians, archivists, and curators at Norfolk Public Library, the University of Virginia, the Library of Congress, the Smithsonian's National Museum of African American History and Culture, Pocahontas Island Black History Museum, Virginia Museum of Fine Arts, and many, many others, without whom this research would not have been possible.

To Kyle Betit, Noah Lapidus, and the Ancestry.com team, who uncovered invaluable information about Minnie and shared with me generations of folks I wouldn't have found on my own.

To Kenneth Pritchett at Central State Hospital for helping me find my grandmother's records.

To my graduate students, Kelsey Orsini and Samantha New, who helped work on research, formatting, and all the moving parts of this book up until the last minute.

To Shanna Crockett and Devyn Casey of Vibe By Design: Creative Solutions, who created the family tree (look for the hidden faces!) and embraced my stories with enthusiasm and vigor.

To Lisa Cain, who lovingly created the book's cover art, first by saying yes, then by asking who Minnie and Mary were and letting me weigh in on the process.

To Jennifer Natalie Fish, for helping with the family photos, for taking my author photo, and for all her selflessness.

To the Sustainable Arts Foundation for their support of working-artist parents.

To Lotus Press, Etruscan Press, Diode Editions, and Beacon Press for ushering words into the world.

To Larissa Melo Pienkowski, seriously, the best agent anyone could ever ask for.

To Matilda Cox and Princess Perry, my Road Dawgs and always editors.

To Honorée Fanonne Jeffers, for all her guidance and encouragement.

To Linda Janet Holmes, whose work on Black midwives and whose voice continue to guide me.

To Natasha Taylor, who'll go on writing trips and sit in libraries with me on a whim, forever friend. To Monica Black, Angela Ferebee, Angel Hall and all the friends who encourage me.

To always in my corner folks: Dante Micheaux, Amanda Johnston, Phillip B. Williams, L. Lamar Wilson, Reginald Dwayne Betts, Christian Campbell, DéLana Dameron, Anita D. Taylor, Jeannie Kim-McPherson, Ada Udechukwu, Eugene Calloway, Cave Canem and the Affrilachian Poets.

To my cousin Ariana Benson, who came back to me as a full-fledged poet and continues to bolster me in our life's work.

To Nicole Reid, Shavon Johnson, Jasmin Rae Francis, and Rashad Williams, cousins who continue to help grow me up.

To my grandmothers: Shirley Bingham, Rebecca Blackburn, Susie Gee, Minnie Fowlkes, Viola Bingham, Loretta Bingham, Mary Knight, Lucy Hyman, and to many others who carried us all.

To my parents, Doris and Robert Bingham, who are always happy being pulled along this zigzagging writerly journey with me. Special thanks to my Mom, the eternal Knight family historian.

To my aunts and uncles on the Knight side: Evelyn, Johnnie, Lawrence, Shirley, Carolyn and Eunice. My Aunts and uncles on the Bingham side: Randy, Ralph, Raymond, Robin, Rosalind and Rhonda. My great aunt Ruth Lucille Suafoa and her daughter, cousin Ruth Lorain Smith. And of course, all my cousins: you are all here in many manifestations. Special thanks to Aunt Rosie and Uncle Radeem, Bingham family historian and caretaker, who also house and feed us whenever we enter on a whim.

To my mother-in-law, Alesia, and brother, Johnathan, for all their love and support.

To my Cute Sweet, always believing, best confidant and secret keeping husband, Michael.

To my children, Michael and Sonsoréa, and grandson, Naveen, for every inspiration.

To the entire Wesleyan team: Suzanna Tamminen, who believed deeply in this work from the very first moment, Stephanie Elliott Prieto, Jaclyn Wilson, Jim Schley, Mindy Basinger Hill, and everyone who had a hand in bringing this book to life.

To all who have sustained me: light and love.

Notes

The book's epigraph is from the WPA narrative of Minnie Lee Fowlkes (indexed as Fulkes) in the Federal Writers' Project: Slave Narrative Project, Vol. 17, Virginia, Berry-Wilson. 1936. Manuscript/Mixed Material. www.loc.gov/item/mesn170/.

On the plantation or, as some say, down home

This poem relies on the text of Minnie's Lee Fowlkes's WPA narrative. In section IV, the italicized lines are from Ephesians 6:5 and Galatians 5:13 in the *New American Bible*.

April when de war surrendered

This title is a line from Minnie's Lee Fowlkes' WPA narrative. www.loc.gov/item/mesn170/.

Work Song

This poem contains a line paraphrased from an interview Susie R. C. Byrd conducted with Ms. Nola (Geneva Fowlkes) Thompson, daughter of Minnie Fowlkes, who said: "The saying is true, 'Sometimes up and sometimes down, Sometimes almost level with the ground.' It seems that all my life has been that." The interview was printed in *Talk About Trouble: A New Deal Portrait of Virginians in the Great Depression*, edited by Nancy J. Martin-Perdue and Charles L. Perdue Jr. (University of North Carolina Press, 1996).

Questions That Still Need Answering

The questions in this poem are taken from the *Questionnaire for Ex-Slaves, Federal Works Project*, reprinted in *Weevils in the Wheat: Interviews with Virginia Ex-Slaves*, edited by Charles L. Perdue Jr., Thomas E. Barden, and Robert K. Phillips (University of Virginia Press, 1976; reprint edition 1991).

RIOTING BREAKS OUT AT NORFOLK, VIRGINIA—Six persons were shot during a clash between whites and blacks in the negro sections of the city tonight. Four of the wounded are negroes, of whom two are expected to die.

This title comes from two articles: "Rioting Breaks Out at Norfolk; Four Shot, None Dead, in Clash As Negro Soldiers Are Welcomed," in the *New-York Tribune*; and "Six Shot in Norfolk Riots," in the *New York Times*; both from July 22, 1919, and found on http://visualizingtheredsummer.com/?dhp-project=archive#.

the Great Depression was hard to distinguish when poverty was always a way of life

The poem's title is taken from the freeservers site "The Great Depression: An African-American Perspective," found at http://mtungsten.freeservers.com/.

Night Class, Peabody High School

This poem is written for Susie R. C. Byrd, a Black educator who lived in Petersburg, Virginia, and who taught night classes for adult learners and served as one of the few Black interviewers for the Works Progress Administration (WPA). She collected stories of those in her community and, hence, many of her narratives are uncharacteristically honest and candid. She interviewed Minnie in 1937, then interviewed Minnie's daughter Geneva for a separate project in 1939. This leads me to believe she may have been a friend of the family.

The Tenderness of One Woman for Another

The poem's title is a line from Mary E. Wilkins Freeman's story "The Tree of Knowledge," referenced in the book *Navigating Women's Friendships in American Literature and Culture*, edited by Kristi Branham and Kelly L. Reames (Palgrave Macmillan, 2022).

victims killed in 1922 were burned at the stake
in a form of torture that most people today
associate with the so-called Dark Ages. These
horrific acts happened in modern [enter the
name of the state where you were born], just
a few generations ago. And white people
caught the events on film and put the photos in
their own family albums

This poem's title and italicized lines in the first stanza are from the article "One family's photo album includes images of a vacation, a wedding anniversary and the lynching of a Black man in Texas," written by Jeffrey L. Littlejohn and published in *The Conversation* on May 3, 2022. See https://theconversation.com/one-familys-photo-album-includes-images-of-a-vacation-a-wedding-anniversary-and-the-lynching-of-a-black-man-in-texas-183704/.

MASTER INDEX: CASE RECORD

Italicized lines are from Martin Anthony Summers, *Madness in the City of Magnificent Intentions: A History of Race and Mental Illness in the Nation's Capital* (Oxford University Press, 2019); also see Summers, "'He Is Psychotic and Always Will Be': Racial Ambivalence and the Limits of Therapeutic Optimism, 1903–1937," in *Madness in the City of Magnificent Intentions* (New York, 2019; online edition, Oxford Academic, 22 Aug. 2019), https://academic.oup.com/book/32411/chapter-abstract/268718486?redirectedFrom=fulltext&login=false/. Boldface words and phrases are quotes or paraphrased from Mary Knight's Central Lunatic Asylum hospital records.

The color blue was full of darkness

This title is a line from the poem "Reading, Dreaming, Hiding" in Kelly Cherry's book *God's Loud Hand* (Louisiana State University Press, 1993).

a fish has broken from the water its rod
of a body

This title is taken from the poem "I Am a Miner. The Light Burns Blue" in Victoria Chang's book *Obit* (Copper Canyon Press, 2020).

Clean white homes and smiling black servants
appropriately attired
in language and dress

This title is taken from Thavolia Glymph's book *Out of the House of Bondage: The Transformation of the Plantation Household* (Cambridge University Press, 2008).

Child With Playthings in Black and White

The poem is based on a photo of Allan Perkins's daughter from the Holsinger Studio Collection, X1858B2, Special Collections, University of Virginia Library.

The Negro Travelers' Green Book, 1957

All italicized lines are from the 1957 edition of the Green Book.

remains of the stained glass windows of the
16th Street Baptist Church

This title is taken from the "Collection Story" at the web page "Lives in Pieces: In memory of Addie Mae Collins, Carol Denise McNair, Cynthia Diane Wesley and Carole Robertson," https://nmaahc.si.edu/explore/stories/lives-pieces/.

Mary Admires James Brown's Casket

This is an echo of Carole Emberton's brilliant insight in her book, *To Walk About In Freedom: The Long Emancipation of Priscilla Joyner* (W. W. Norton, 2022), in which she says: "The cursory fashion with which most enslaved people were put to rest, the absence of reverence or ceremony, the unceasing nature of slave labor that denied any time for grieving, the lack of control enslaved people had over the burial of their kin—these conditions shaped how the charter generation and the generations to come viewed funerals. The desire for a better send-off, even for a grand display of respect and love, would not be seen as a wasteful extravagance. The ever-present threat of violence and death that has haunted Black people since slavery has shaped their relationship to death and their funerary practices, resulting in a culture that expects death and celebrates the dead in ways that white culture does not appreciate" (153).

There is going to be a resurrection of both the righteous and unrighteous

This title is taken from Acts 24:15 in the *New World Translation of the Holy Scriptures* (Study Edition, 2013), published by the Watchtower Bible and Tract Society.

Commemorative Headdress For Her Journey Beyond Heaven

This title is taken from Kenya Robinson's art piece "Commemorative Headdress From Her Journey Beyond Heaven," housed in the National Museum of African American History and Culture (NMAAHC).

White Children and the Intimate Landscape of Defeat

This title is taken from Catherine A. Jones's book *Intimate Reconstructions: Children in Postemancipation Virginia* (University of Virginia Press, 2015).

The black mammy, like the southern lady, was also born in the white mind

This title is taken from *The New Encyclopedia of Southern Culture, Volume 4: Myth, Manners, and Memory*, edited by Charles Reagan Wilson (University of North Carolina Press, 2014).

25 days after I am born

This poem is written for Beulah Mae Donald. The italicized line is from Ronald Reagan's presidential inaugural address, given on January 20, 1981. See https://avalon.law.yale.edu/20th_century/reagan1.asp/.

because the scale of our breathing is planetary, at the very least

This poem takes cues from theories in Stephen Hawking's book *A Brief History of Time from the Big Bang to Black Holes* (Bantam, 1988); and from Alexis Pauline Gumbs's *Undrowned: Black Feminist Lessons from Marine Mammals* (AK Press, 2020), from which the title and italicized lines are quoted.

The Domestic who is the Bearer of the Present

This title is taken from Elisabeth Celnart's book *The Gentleman and Lady's Book of Politeness and Propriety of Deportment (*Allen and Ticknor, 1833).

The *Lose Your Mother* Suite

Italicized headings are excerpted from "Prologue: The Path of Strangers" and "Fugitive Dreams" in Saidiya Hartman's *Lose Your Mother: A Journey Along the Atlantic Slave Route* (© 2007 Saidiya Hartman; reprinted by permission of Farrar, Straus and Giroux; All Rights Reserved). Sonnet XVI, "Saidiya's Cento," is composed of the quoted section titles. In Sonnet XIII, the line attributed to Nikky Finney is from her poem "Left" in *Head Off & Split* (TriQuarterly, 2011).

Where did you come from/how did you arrive?

This title is taken from Bhanu Kapil's book *The Vertical Interrogation of Strangers* (Kelsey Street Press, 2001).

Refusing Rilke's *You must change your life*

Part of the poem's title is from Rainer Maria Rilke's poem "Archaic Torso of Apollo" (phrased as quoted in various translations).

I am trying to carve out a world where people are not the sum total of their disaster

This title is a paraphrase of a line uttered by Sarah M. Broom, author of *The Yellow House*, in a conversation with Kiese Laymon, author of *Heavy*, which was streamed live on July 16, 2020, by #BNEvents Live (#BNEvents); see the yellow house with sarah m. broom in conversation with kiese laymon, www.youtube.com/watch?v=073XxCmKk-4/.

Illustration Credits

pages xvi and xvii
Family tree image created by Vibe By Design: Creative Solutions (2022).

page 4
The photo was taken at the Library of Virginia. Photo courtesy of the author.

page 18
Du Bois, W. E. B., collector. [*African Americans, mostly women, sorting tobacco at the T. C. Williams & Co., tobacco, Richmond, Virginia.*] Photograph. [1899?]. Library of Congress call number LOT 11302 [item] [P&P]. Repository: Library of Congress Prints and Photographs Division, http://hdl.loc.gov/loc.pnp/pp.print/.

page 23
Photo courtesy of the author.

page 27
Wolcott, Marion Post, photographer. [Untitled photo, possibly related to: *Coal miner, his wife and two of their children (note child's legs). Bertha Hill, West Virginia.*] Photograph. 1938. Library of Congress call number LC-USF33-030206-M4 [P&P]. Repository: Library of Congress Prints and Photographs Division, http://hdl.loc.gov/loc.pnp/pp.print/.

page 32
Eisenman, George A., photographer. "Northeast view. Old Farmers' Market, West Old & Rock Streets, Petersburg, Petersburg (Independent City), VA," from *The Cockade City* (Petersburg: Geo. M Englebrecht, 1894), 24. Library of Congress reproduction number HABS VA,27-PET,26--1. Repository: Library of Congress Prints and Photographs Division, http://hdl.loc.gov/loc.pnp/pp.print/.

page 35
Delano, Jack, photographer. *Saturday afternoon in Union Point, Greene County, Georgia*. Photograph. 1941. Library of Congress call number LC-USF33-020981-M1. Repository: Farm Security Administration: Office of War Information Photograph Collection (Library of Congress). Repository: Library of Congress Prints and Photographs Division, http://hdl.loc.gov/loc.pnp/pp.print/.

page 44
Photo courtesy of the author.

page 51
Central State Hospital ledger. The photo was taken in the Library of Virginia archives. Photo courtesy of the author.

page 57
Davis Bottom, Superintendent Public Printing. *Building for chronically ill females*. 45th Annual Report of Central State Hospital Petersburg, Virginia. Photo in the public domain via Wikimedia Commons: https://commons.wikimedia.org/wiki/File:Chronic-female-csh.jpg/.

page 61
Holsinger, Rufus W., photographer. "Hazelhurst Bolton Perkins (1911–1923)." (Miss Allan Perkins, daughter of Mr. Allan Perkins.) Holsinger Studio Special Collections, University of Virginia. https://search.lib.virginia.edu/sources/images/items/uva-lib:1041488/.

page 64
November 17, 1955. *The News and Observer* documented the African American neighborhood in Raleigh, North Carolina, just south of Memorial Auditorium, locally known as Southside. From the N&O negative collection, State Archives of North Carolina,

Raleigh, NC. Photo used with permission granted by *The News and Observer*.

page 66
Photographer unknown. "'Daddy' Grace's Fourth of July Parade, 1958: Norfolk, Virginia." Sargeant Memorial Collection Digital Collection, Norfolk Public Library, https://cdm15987.contentdm.oclc.org/digital/collection/p15987coll9/id/1002/rec/215/. Photo used with permission of the Norfolk Public Library.

page 69
Photo courtesy of the author.

page 85
Photo courtesy of the author.

page 97
Photo courtesy of the author.

page 113
Photo courtesy of the author.

Selected Bibliography

Barden, Thomas E., et al., editors. *Weevils in the Wheat: Interviews with Virginia Ex-Slaves*. University of Virginia Press, 1976.

Byrd, Ayana, and Lori Tharps. *Hair Story: Untangling the Roots of Black Hair in America*. St. Martin's Griffin, 2014.

Costa, Tom. "The Geography of Slavery in Virginia," 2005, digital collection hosted by the University of Virginia, www2.vcdh.virginia.edu/gos/.

———. "Runaway Slaves and Servants in Colonial Virginia." *Encyclopedia Virginia*, Virginia Humanities, 12 Jan. 2021, www.encyclopediavirginia.org/entries/runaway-slaves-and-servants-in-colonial-virginia/.

Curwood, Anastasia Carol. *Stormy Weather Middle-Class African American Marriages between the Two World Wars*. University of North Carolina Press, 2010.

Dismal Swamp Canal Welcome Center, website hosted by Camden County, North Carolina, www.dismalswampwelcomecenter.com/.

Emberton, Carole. *To Walk about in Freedom the Long Emancipation of Priscilla Joyner*. W. W. Norton, 2022.

Federal Writers' Project: Slave Narrative Project, Vol. 17, Virginia, Berry-Wilson. 1936. Manuscript/Mixed Material. Accessed through the Library of Congress, www.loc.gov/item/mesn170/.

Fry, Gladys-Marie. *The Night Riders: A Study in the Social Control of the Negro*. University of North Carolina Press, 2001.

Gumbs, Alexis Pauline. *Dub: Finding Ceremony*. Duke University Press, 2020.

———. *Undrowned: Black Feminist Lessons from Marine Mammals*. AK Press, 2020.

Hartman, Saidiya V. *Lose Your Mother: A Journey along the Atlantic Slave Route*. Farrar, Straus and Giroux, 2007.

———. *Wayward Lives, Beautiful Experiments: Intimate Histories of Social Upheaval*. W. W. Norton, 2019.

Hawking, Stephen. *A Brief History of Time from the Big Bang to Black Holes*. Bantam, 1988.

Henderson, William D. *Gilded Age City Politics, Life, and Labor in Petersburg, Virginia, 1874–1889*. University Press of America, 1980.

"History of Slavery in Virginia." In *History of American Women*, 2008, www.womenhistoryblog.com/2008/07/slavery-in-virginia.html.

Huddleston, John. *Killing Ground Photographs of the Civil War and the Changing American Landscape*. Johns Hopkins University Press, 2002.

Lebsock, Suzanne. *The Free Women of Petersburg: Status and Culture in a Southern Town, 1784–1860*. W. W. Norton, 1985.

Lost Friends Database. The Historic New Orleans Collection, 2016, hosted by the Williams Research Center, www.hnoc.org/database/lost-friends/index.html/.

Martin-Perdue, Nancy J., and Charles L. Perdue Jr., editors. *Talk About Trouble: A New Deal Portrait of Virginians in the Great Depression*. University of North Carolina Press, 1996.

Mitchell, Mary Niall. *Raising Freedom's Child: Black Children and Visions of the Future after Slavery*. New York University Press, 2008.

Roosevelt, Franklin D. "May 27, 1941: Fireside Chat 17: On an Unlimited National Emergency." *Miller Center*, https://millercenter.org/the-presidency/presidential-speeches/may-27-1941-fireside-chat-17-unlimited-national-emergency/.

Sachs, Aaron. "Stumps in the Wilderness." In *The Blue, the Gray, and the Green: Toward an Environmental History of the Civil War*, edited by Brian Allen Drake. University of Georgia Press, 2015.

Sayers, Daniel O. *A Desolate Place for a Defiant People: The Archaeology of Maroons, Indigenous Americans, and Enslaved Laborers in the Great Dismal Swamp.* University Press of Florida, 2014.

Schweninger, Loren, and Franklin, John Hope. *Runaway Slaves: Rebels on the Plantation.* Oxford University Press, 2000.

Schomburg Center for Research in Black Culture, Manuscripts, Archives and Rare Books Division, New York Public Library. "The Negro Travelers' Green Book: 1957." The New York Public Library Digital Collections. 1957. https://digitalcollections.nypl.org/items/089a5a60-848f-0132-a7aa-58d385a7b928

Smith, Barbara Ellen. *Neither Separate nor Equal Women, Race, and Class in the South.* Temple University Press, 1999.

Smith, Tom W. "Changing Racial Labels: From 'Colored' to 'Negro' to 'Black' to 'African American.'" *The Public Opinion Quarterly* 56, no. 4, 1992, 496–514. JSTOR, http://www.jstor.org/stable/2749204. Accessed 21 Dec. 2022.

Snead, James A. "On Repetition in Black Culture." *African American Review* 50.4 (2017): 648–56.

Summers, Martin. *Madness in the City of Magnificent Intentions: A History of Race and Mental Illness in the Nation's Capital.* Oxford University Press, 2019.

Towner, Betsy. "How the Civil War Changed Your Life." AARP.org, 2001, www.aarp.org/politics-society/history/info-04-2011/8-ways-civil-war-changed-lives.html/.

Townsend, George Alfred. *Campaigns of a Non-Combatant, and His Romaunt Abroad During the War.* Blelock, 1866. Accessed through Google Books.

"Tulsa Race Riot a Lesson That Must Be Learned." *Tulsa World,* 4 Jun. 2011, www.tulsaworld.com/news/local/racemassacre/tulsa-race-riot-a-lesson-that-must-be-learned/article_12e7e077-d01a-52c1-bc35-72a50c1bddb1.html/.

Virginia Writers' Program. *The Negro in Virginia.* John F. Blair, Publisher, 1994.

Wallace, Eric J. "Bright Leaf Legacy." *Virginia Living,* 7 Nov. 2018, www.virginialiving.com/culture/bright-leaf-legacy/.

White, Shane, and Graham J. White. *The Sounds of Slavery: Discovering African American History through Songs, Sermons, and Speech.* Beacon Press, 2005.

Williams, Heather Andrea. *Help Me to Find My People: The African American Search for Family Lost in Slavery.* University of North Carolina Press, 2012.

About the Author

Remica Bingham-Risher, a native of Phoenix, Arizona, is an alumna of Old Dominion University and Bennington College. She is a Cave Canem fellow and Affrilachian Poet. Her work has been published in the *New York Times*, the *Writer's Chronicle*, *New Letters*, *Callaloo*, and *Essence*, among other publications. She is the author of *Conversion* (Lotus, 2006), winner of the Naomi Long Madgett Poetry Award; *What We Ask of Flesh* (Etruscan, 2013), shortlisted for the Hurston/Wright Award; and *Starlight & Error* (Diode, 2017), winner of the Diode Editions Book Award. Her first book of prose is *Soul Culture: Black Poets, Books and Questions that Grew Me Up* (Beacon Press, 2022). She is currently the director of Quality Enhancement Plan Initiatives at Old Dominion University and resides in Norfolk, Virginia, with her husband and children. www.remicabinghamrisher.com, IG: @remicawriter.